I0763513

Black Heart
BLACK CELL

Black Heart/Black Cell

ISBN: 978-1-7378736-2-4 (hardback)
978-1-7378736-0-0 (paperback)
978-1-7378736-1-7 (ebook)

Printed in the United States of America

Black Heart
BLACK CELL

A Jeannie Loomis Novel

GARY J. ROSE

My thanks once again to Mike Lake for doing the first read, offering advice, and inspiring me to complete this novel which seemed more difficult to compose than other Jeannie Loomis novels. Perhaps it seemed more of a challenge because I recently lost my mom, who championed my writing and had been my first reader.

I would be remiss if I did not thank John Maghuyop, who creates outstanding covers to complement my book titles.

Special thanks are extended to Drs. Jane and Fred Vallier of Vallier Editing for another great job of editing.

In life, we do things. Some we wish we had never done. Some we wish we could replay a million times in our heads. But they all make us who we are. And, in the end, they shape every detail about us. If we were to reverse any of them, we wouldn't be the person we are.

So just live. Make mistakes. Have wonderful memories. But never ever second guess who you are, where you have been, and most importantly, where it is you're going.

—Unknown

What readers are saying about the Jeannie Loomis novels:

Ark of the Covenant

Based on the title, I was expecting a more Indiana Jones-like story. And while it is in some regard (like the title, right??), I really got a "Tomb Raider" vibe while reading the whole book. Like seriously, after a few character and plot changes, this could be a legit screenplay for a Tomb Raider movie or video game. Hats off to the author for a rollercoaster ride of a novel.

Star Chamber

This well-written thriller really draws you in quickly with excellent character development, fast-paced action, and good writing. The protagonist is a flawed and driven woman whose life has been devoted to justice, leaving her without children or a mate. FBI Agent Jeannie Loomis has unfinished business, and even a conspiracy of epic proportions won't stop her. Hard to put this one down. When you're finished, you'll be wanting more from the series.

Forgotten Plans

I'm a sucker for thrillers and FBI crime stories, and this one hit the nail on the head. I loved the plot which you can relate to, especially if you clearly remember the events on 9-11. The setting is fabulous because how can you possibly go wrong with San Francisco for a thriller? You can't. And Jeannie, well, I just loved Jeannie. She's a smart, strong female FBI agent who reminded me a lot of Clarice from Silence of The Lambs, who I also adore. Probably one of the better thrillers I've read this year, and I thought the political/religious language added some sustenance to the story. This novel should be on the best seller list.

House of Special Purpose

This is my fourth Jeannie Loomis novel, and I have enjoyed each one. The Loomis novels are fast-paced and page-turners. The crises that Jeannie and her team face are very relevant to our society today. It has all the ingredients for a top-notch thriller. References back to the assassination of the last Czar of Russia, the royal jewels, and an urban terrorist group. Hollywood needs to make more movies with plots like this book.

Time Game

The 5th Jeannie Loomis novel in its series, Time Game is an intriguing story that avoids the pitfalls of its well-worn subject matter by always managing to add an unexpected twist or two. For those that read like me, and those that don't - but enjoy a good out-of-the-ordinary good guys vs bad guys story - I highly recommend.

Thin Blue Line

This was my first Jeanne Loomis novel, though from what I understand they stand on their own pretty well. After reading it, it will not be my last. It gives a rather believable picture of crime and law enforcement in the San Francisco area and is quite fast-paced and engaging. It was funny at times too. A fun and intriguing work of police fiction.

The Fourth Reich

This book's jarring content is well woven into a frighteningly well-conceived plot that cleverly brings the wickedness of the Third Reich into a new chapter where the terror of a Fourth Reich is dawning as wheels turn and experiments push forward towards a new Nazi power. It is well written, fast paced and all and all a very entertaining read. I would however advise caution as its content may not be for sensitive readers, or especially those who experienced the horrors of the concentration camps of WWII firsthand.

Other books by the author:

JEANNIE LOOMIS NOVELS:

Ark of the Covenant – Raid on the Church of Our Lady Mary of Zion

Star Chamber

Forgotten Plans

House of Special Purpose

Time Game

Thin Blue Line

The Fourth Reich

NON-FICTION:

Hitting Rock Bottom

Towards the Integration of Police Psychology Techniques to Combat Juvenile Delinquency in K-12 Classrooms

Teaching Inside the Walls

How To Create A Public School Military Style Boot-Camp Academy

Preface

THE 2020 CENSUS showed that California experienced its slowest growth rate ever during the 2010s, a slowdown so severe the state lost a seat in the House of Representatives. It was part of a decades-long trend; the consequence of fewer births, more deaths, a slowing of international migration, and—capturing a great deal of attention—a large migration out of California to other states due to its government's liberal policies, high taxes, homelessness, and relatively high cost of living. Over decades, this migration has the power to reshape the state. During the 2010s, about 6.1 million people moved from California to other states, while only 4.9 million moved into California from other parts of the U.S.

One individual who left California and opted to live in Idaho had an additional reason for the move.

He found the second largest chunk of untamed, roadless wilderness in the contiguous U.S.—2.4 million acres of rough terrain; a natural place to hide hideous deeds.

According to 2021 geographic calculations, the most remote spot in the entire continental U.S. borders Idaho and Nevada in Owyhee County. But there is only one place that holds the title of the most isolated spot in the state fully contained in Idaho, and that's an area accessible only by plane or experienced hikers, unmarred by trails, and completely hidden from any road.

For the killer, the Frank Church-River of No Return Wilderness is so vast and untouched that adventuring through the diverse landscape is like a trip back in time. Virgin pine trees dot the mountainsides as far as the eye can see. Not even the notoriously wild Salmon River navigates through this rugged landscape. A person would be hard-pressed to find another human for miles, and that is why he loves it so much. A man with a black heart, comfortable in his killing fields.

***

Unseen worlds exist within our world, worlds beneath what we call cyberspace, worlds protected by firewalls, passwords, and the most advanced security systems. In one of these worlds, we hide our deepest secrets, our most incriminating information, and, of course, a whole lot of money. It's a super hacker's dream.

Over the past decade, ransomware has evolved into an ongoing security threat for organizations worldwide. As companies have gone increasingly digital, cybercriminals have sought to maximize their profits by exploiting the vulnerabilities that come with a rapidly expanding ecosystem.

More recently, ransomware attacks have increased at an alarming rate, with victims ranging from one of the largest fuel suppliers in the U.S. to Ireland's Department of Health. But one of the world's top Black Hats wants something more. He is not just interested in reaping billions of dollars from the world's elite; he is also interested in their downfall. His Black Cell organization will realign the "haves" and the "have-nots."

Early Summer 2018

SHE TRIED TO ignore the pain in her right knee after her second fall. The sharp gravel scraped away her skin, and she could feel blood running down her leg into her tennis shoe. She felt more blood dripping from her nose, which seemed to have taken the full impact of one of her falls, being unable to brace herself with her hands zip-tied behind her back. Rubbing her head against a tree, she managed to tear away part of the cloth over her eyes, barely allowing any sunlight in. The terrain was covered with scrub brush, berry bushes, and trees. She ran uphill, across small streams, fell, and rolled into ravines, and yet he still seemed to be gaining ground on her.

She was a hopeful young model trying to break into the Hollywood scene like so many other young adults. She believed her blond shoulder-length hair, haunting green eyes, and killer body would take her far. Occasionally, she stopped to catch her breath but would soon hear his footsteps behind her again on the deer trail. She knew her fate if he caught up with her. She was the prey, and he was the hunter.

Mother told me there are no easy roads in life. You've got to work hard to get ahead, but I didn't listen. I wanted everything now, not tomorrow. What will my mom do if he kills me? We lost my dad only a year ago. She needs me. Please, God, forgive me and save me from this crazy man. How could I have been so stupid, she wondered as she ran farther into the forest.

Her gut told her something was off with the older man who had approached her, offering her a position with his photography firm that would lead to a modeling job. The allure of a great modeling position overcame her instincts. *He promised me that with a professional portfolio and a little coaching he would provide, I'd be on the fast track to becoming a top model and Hollywood starlet.*

Sandy could tell that she was on an incline, and it was draining what little was left of her strength. She summoned all the energy she had left and reached the top of the grade, only to lose her footing and fall. She gave it her last effort and stood up.

***

This one's fast. She made good use of the thirty-minute head start, he said to himself. This was not his first hunt. In fact, he honestly couldn't remember how many successful hunts he'd been on, but his diary listed detailed names, dates, mementos, and final resting places of "the game." It had all started in Alaska.

Law enforcement had paid little attention to him up there. They were more concerned with poachers, illegal hunting, prostitution, and crime in Eskimo boroughs. Missing females were usually the ones "who had just left town." The likes of the Green River Killer, Gary Ridgway, Charles Manson, and even Charles Ng seemed to be fading memories to the new breed of police officers.

Shit, most of those pussies have never even fought in a war. My grandfather fought in Vietnam. When he was in high school, he and the other eighteen-year-old males worried about being drafted and getting their asses shot off in the jungle. Not today's snowflakes. Shit, most still live in the basement of their mommy and daddy's house. This bitch has more pure instinct than any modern-day cop.

The rifle shot entered the back of her head, and the bullet never exited her skull. She was dead before she hit the ground.

He stood over her body, admiring his shot. He turned her over and noticed the gold heart pendant around her neck. He reached down and grabbed the chain, ripping the necklace from her throat. *You were the best so far.*

2020

Chapter One

"I'M TELLING YOU. The worst career move I ever made was letting you guys talk me into becoming president of the police officers' association. The first time I took on the chief, he made it clear that he'd be looking out for my personal career. In other words, "I'm going to fuck you over every chance I get,"' Jim said as he spat a wad of tobacco on the ground next to some dried-up leaves and rubbed his boot heel in it.

"You know what they say, Jim, the road to a strong police officers' association is riddled with the corpses of dead association presidents. The association needed someone strong and respected enough by the troops to take on that dictatorial asshole. Let's just relax up here, get us an elk, and forget about all that political crap back at the department," Ron replied as he scratched at his beard and gazed out over the valley.

Patches of snow covered the ground. With such a light winter, more ground was exposed than was covered with snow, making it easy to maneuver through the tough terrain. Some of the pines had a fresh dusting on them, but that was all. They had already set up a base camp before setting out for the day.

A fifteen-year veteran of the police force, Jim Jamerson, was Hunter's patrol sergeant and friend. They became members of the force on the same day, attended the same law enforcement academy, and, from day one, enjoyed each other's comradery.

Officer Ron Hunter never showed a sign of being upset when Jamerson beat him in the sergeant's exam and was now his supervisor. He remained easygoing, chill, and just happy he was receiving a paycheck and enjoying his job. He followed orders yet liked that Jamerson used him as a sounding board. Jim raised his hand, motioning for Hunter to remain still and not giving him a chance to respond. He pointed to a grouping of trees south of a small meadow. "I think I saw something."

Both Jim and Ron loved big game hunting when not fishing. This was a major reason both their parents had decided to leave Arizona and relocate to Idaho. They both referred to their new state as God's country: hundreds of lakes and streams teeming with trophy fish and forests filled with big game. Sure, a person had to put up with snow and miserable weather for a few months of the year, but neither of them would trade it nor entertain thoughts of returning to the Grand Canyon state.

Their parents had been friends for years near Scottsdale, and both Ron and Jim decided it best for their future families to grow up outside the desert. They had vacillated between Montana, Washington, Oregon, and Idaho. Based on their political beliefs, which leaned heavily toward conservatism, they quickly eliminated Oregon and Washington before settling on Idaho. Both Ron and Jim attended the same elementary, middle, and high schools, and both played football and baseball--one better than the other, depending on the sport.

During the silence that followed, Jim listened carefully. He was no stranger to the outdoors, and he was certainly not a man who was afraid of much. He surveyed the area again before turning to Ron, "Sorry. Thought we had ourselves an elk." They were a few miles inside the Frank Church-River of No Return, a wilderness of steep, rugged mountains, deep canyons, and wild, whitewater rivers. The Salmon River Mountains were to the south--a massive range that dominated the wilderness, and the Salmon River Canyon was one of the deepest gorges in North America, even deeper than the famous Grand Canyon of Colorado and Arizona.

As they continued their way into the dense forest, Ron tripped over something buried under pine needles. Gaining his balance and being pissed with his clumsiness, he looked down at something he quickly recognized as a human skull. “Oh, shit!” he said, drawing Jim’s attention. Knowing from their professional training not to disturb the area, they were still able to see a femur and a partial rib cage from their standing positions.

“Definitely human,” Jim said. “Take out your satellite phone and call it in. Let’s do a cursory search and then head back to base camp. No one will get here until tomorrow.” Scouting the area leading away from their find, they discovered more remains. “Got a hand and a foot. Damned animals have spread shit all over the place.” Both officers took pictures of the crime scene on their cellphones so they could accurately describe how they found the body, then headed back to camp.

Ron was right. A three-member forensic team from the ISP would not arrive until mid-afternoon the next day. Even in great weather, it was still a hellish hike to get to this portion of the Frank Church-River of No Return. Ron and Jim finished lunch and made a fresh pot of coffee, then waited for the forensic team. When the team arrived, they were ready for coffee. Ron poured each a cup with a trembling hand. When Jim noticed, he shot Ron an accusing look and proceeded to tell forensic what he knew.

“Saw a femur in the dirt; called it in.’

“When was that?” A team member asked.

"I don't know exactly. What do you think, Ron? 08:15 hours or so?"

"Yeah, that sounds about right. It was before 09:00."

Finishing their coffee, they escorted the team to the crime scene, giving statements as they went. Having turned the scene over to the evidence team, they were instructed to contact the ISP in Coeur d'Alene when they got out of the wilderness the next day in case more questions needed answering. They still hoped to bag an elk.

***

Assistant Special Agent in Charge (ASAC), Jeannie Loomis, currently on a much-needed vacation at her cabin above Lake Coeur d'Alene, awoke with a male hand on her right breast. Another arm was under her pillow. She stirred only slightly and, with her movement, felt the rise of his penis next to her ass. She smiled and turned to face her lover, Interpol Agent Sean Delaney.

"Good morning, Agent Delaney."

"Good morning to you, Agent Loomis."

He returned his hand to her breast and placed his other hand behind her neck, stroking her long hair. She reached down and found his waiting erection. "And what do we have here?" She asked.

"I don't know. You're a highly trained FBI agent. Perhaps you should investigate," he said in his British accent.

Fifteen minutes later, the two were in the shower making plans for the day. Delaney was first to finish dressing and told Jeannie to take her time. He wanted to make a special breakfast for them.

"Fish and chips?" she asked.

"Bloody hell, no! I'm thinking French toast, bacon, sausage, and a hot cup of tea. By the way, Ismail got me hooked on his Portuguese sausage--linguiça."

"God, I love your accent," came her response.

Ismail Flores was Jeannie's second in command. He was not just her co-worker; he was her best friend. Together, they had solved several high-profile investigations. He sat at the hospital after she got shot during a shootout at one of their field offices. His family was her family since both her mom and dad had already passed on.

Slightly younger than Jeannie, they shared the same political views and loved to tease each other whenever the opportunity presented itself. He loved to boast about his Portuguese nationality; both his grandparents came from Portugal's Azores. Standing 5'10" with a well-groomed mustache and male pattern baldness, he always seemed to create energy upon entering a room. Jeannie used him as a sounding board when the job's stresses and frustrations got to her.

Jeannie often thought that without Ismail, she would never have advanced as rapidly as she had in the bureau. When she took the ASAC position at the San Francisco bureau, she requested that he be transferred to the City-By-The-Bay; an offer he quickly accepted.

They were friends who agreed, on rare occasions, to disagree, but it was frightening how they both seemed to agree 99% of the time. Neither were thin-skinned or afraid to cross over into gray areas while attempting to solve a case. Both had killed on the job, and neither seemed to bat an eyelid over their actions. All cops would lay down their lives for their brother law enforcement comrades, but Jeannie felt her career would end if Ismail were killed in the line of duty.

They did not keep secrets from each other until, for some unknown reason, Jeannie hid her recent inheritance from an unknown aunt. She had fallen in love and was engaged to Ismail's cousin, NSA agent Ricky Pinheiro, who had been killed in a shootout with an urban terrorist group.

Ismail humorously called Delaney "James Bond, Mr. 007" behind his back when teasing Jeannie about her new boyfriend. Jeannie had tried to deny the relationship with Sean but finally relented, knowing that Ismail just wanted her to be happy.

Jeannie dried her hair while thinking about the great night and morning of lovemaking and how she had first met Sean. A former black ops military unit called the Banshees, led by Frank Silva, believed they knew the location of the genuine Ark of the Covenant religious relic. Jeannie and her team collaborated with Interpol, where Sean was the bureau chief. Unfortunately for both agencies, the investigation literally blew up in their faces with the loss of all identified suspects.

Her thoughts then drifted to her second run-in with Sean, which ultimately led to them becoming lovers. A relative of the infamous Joseph Mengele, the Angel of Death at Auschwitz, had secretly continued genetic experiments in the hope of creating a new Reich, the Fourth Reich. Mengele's organization was responsible for kidnapping several young look-a-like females whose appearances exemplified their sought-after Aryan characteristics.

While Jeannie and Sean had attempted to locate the kidnapped females, as well as capture the SS doctor, she herself was abducted. She and Sean already felt a spark of attraction before the Nazi investigation got rolling. *Not your typical romantic meeting, was it?* She thought.

Sean was taller than Jeannie at 6'1" and of average weight. He had closely groomed dark hair and brown eyes that complimented a chiseled smooth-shaven face. Besides loving his British accent, Jeannie loved his ability to inject humor into their discussions; it was typical British humor with a strong element of satire aimed at the absurdity of everyday life, often delivered deadpan with a straight face.

Sean had a lot of pluses: he was fun to be with, loved to laugh at life, appeared responsible, and had an important job. But if there were one thing Jeannie did not like, and it was possibly a red flag, it was a sense of secrecy. Jeannie could not put her finger on what seemed off with Sean. She felt perhaps he harbored a darker side--a reticent nature of his being.

Sean lost his wife to cancer several years earlier, and they had no children. Was it losing his wife that made him seem distant at times? Or maybe it was his job. Although it was similar to Jeannie's duties with the FBI, he didn't seem to have to go into the field as much as she did. Perhaps this was what caused occasional tension between them, yet neither brought it up. Could their current romantic interludes be heading for marriage? *Maybe someday he will open up,* she thought.

Chapter Two

HER CABIN HAD once been owned by the head of the Banshee's, Frank Silva. When he and his crew went missing, Jeannie reached out to a local realtor asking to be notified if the cabin became listed. It was a sprawling, two-story log cabin, much too big for Jeannie, but she loved its setting in the hills above Lake Coeur d'Alene.

"It can only go up in value, especially with all those Californians relocating," the real estate agent told her when it came on the market, and in the short time she had owned it, it had increased in value tremendously. *The real estate market is out of control,* she told herself.

After taking possession, Jeannie searched the cabin and grounds from top to bottom, hoping to find some evidence of the planned Ark of the Covenant heist.

But, like the FBI evidence team that searched months earlier, she found nothing.

At the time, she was just a field agent with no supervisory responsibilities. Months were spent monitoring Frank Silva and his gang of rogue soldiers' movements and Nancy, a biblical historian professor who believed she knew the Ark of the Covenant's exact location.

Mysteriously, everyone Jeannie's team had been monitoring suddenly vanished with no trace. Jeannie was stunned and could not give up, even traveling on her own dime to Ethiopia to see the chapel that allegedly held the Ark, only to find the chapel undisturbed and revealing nothing.

Sometimes, she had a hard time moving past unsolved cases. She remembered her godfather, a former thirty-year member of the San Francisco Police Department, who, even years after retirement, continued investigating cold cases on his own time. He told her, "It's like an itch you can't get rid of." She wondered if it were just because she was super competitive. Had growing up around her godfather and hearing him gloat over successfully solving cases subconsciously driven her to follow a case until it was brought to a successful conclusion? Or maybe, it was simply not wanting to let a suspect escape justice if catching them could bring closure for victims.

"How was your shower?" Sean asked as Jeannie finally made it to the kitchen, where she found a hot cup of tea waiting on the granite counter.

"It was great when you were with me," she replied with a slight blush. "God, that smells so great. You're spoiling me."

"So, after breakfast, what's on our agenda today?" he asked, plating two pieces of French toast, bacon, a slice of linguiça, and scrambled eggs and then sliding it toward Jeannie. "The weather looks splendid."

"Boy, when I get back, I'll have to work double-time at the gym. But I'm not complaining," she replied, putting butter and syrup on her French toast. "Well, since you seem to love driving my new car, I thought we'd start out driving around the lake, and I can be your Idaho tour guide. Lake Coeur d'Alene is one of the largest natural bodies of water in Idaho. There are tons of campgrounds, hiking trails, and beaches lining the 25 miles of shoreline." In a flirtatious British accent, she said, "And if you fancy, you can take in any of the popular activities like jet skiing, fishing, kite surfing—you name it. Just stop anytime you see something your heart desires."

"God, I love your English accent," Sean said with a broad smile. "And who wouldn't want to drive your Corvette. I still don't see many 2020 models on the road, even in San Francisco. The FBI must pay well."

Jeannie just smiled while cutting her linguiça. Her thoughts turned to Ismail, who, if he saw them both eating his favorite Portuguese sausage, would be clapping. She also thought of the secret she had not shared with anyone, not even Ismail, that she had inherited a ton of money from an unknown aunt whom, until being notified by her aunt's estate attorney, she never knew existed. She learned there had been some type of falling out between her aunt and her mom, which she would investigate when time permitted.

The bigger question she asked herself was why was she concealing the fact? She was mercilessly teased when she showed up at the bureau driving a new Corvette, including comments like, "Wow, someone must be on the take," or, "God, the FBI must pay really well!" They were all in good nature, but Jeannie soon tired of it and began to simply say she decided to use the life insurance money her parents had left her, plus her take of their estate.

Maybe it was because she felt people might not take her seriously if they knew she had a ton of money. Would people think she bought her way to the top? Since the bureau's glass ceiling had been breached only a short time before, she was sure someone would think she had not legitimately earned her rank. She doubted people would come out of the woodwork soliciting money from her, but she could not be certain of that. *But why keep it from my closest friends and colleagues, Ismail and the SAC? Perhaps in time,* she thought.

She loved the look of the new Corvette, and along with her older Vette trade-in, she purchased it with cash, shocking the car salesman. The only thing she did not like about her new car was that it was not offered with a manual transmission that would allow her to run through the gears. She told herself she wasn't getting any younger, so an automatic would be fine.

Returning to her best British accent, she continued, "The north side of the lake is the area most developed for tourists. We can start out driving through that. Each winter, there's a wildlife spectacle on the lake when hundreds of bald eagles fly in to feed on spawning Kokanee salmon. You wouldn't believe how many people flock there with their cameras or cellphones and photograph it. No pun intended.

"The whole area's overrun with shopping, dining, and live entertainment for tourists. Most locals stay away in the summer months. Something's always happening in the downtown Coeur d'Alene streets, and, of course, the beautiful waterfront backdrop adds to the excitement. The downtown area has over 100 retail stores, including specialty boutiques, fine art galleries, and antique shops. Naturally, everything's overpriced." She laughed and dropped the accent. They had reached their comfort zone.

Delaney smiled at her, then reached over and tucked a strand of hair behind her ear. However, Jeannie sensed that Delaney was not hearing her, as though he were somewhere else.

"We can go to Mineral Ridge east of the city center. It overlooks Beauty Bay and the Lake. It's a historic, scenic area with a fantastic national recreation trail. I hiked it, and it was well worth the effort. The trail goes up all the way to the ridge with switchbacks, and, as you'd expect, there're interpretive markers along the trail that, along with a guidebook, describe the flora, fauna, and history of the recreation site. Sorry, I bet I sound like a tour guide."

"Not at all. You really seem to enjoy the area, and from what I've seen so far, I'll love it too. The air up here is so clean, and I love the smell of pine. Let's finish breakfast, and while you get ready for our little jaunt around the pond, I'll load the dishwasher."

"Around the pond?" Jeannie laughed. "Wait until you see the size of this pond, buddy."

Jeannie decided to dress in layers on top since she knew that later that afternoon, the weather would really warm up. However, she wore shorts and a pair of white sandals. *Girl still has to look sexy for her man.* Leaving the master bathroom after a final look, she headed for the stairs and heard Sean talking to someone. At first, she thought he was on his cell, but from the top of the stairs, she could see two men at the front door.

"Jeannie, these two officers are from the Idaho State Police," Sean said as he motioned for them to enter.

"Agent Loomis, I'm Detective Sergeant Max Elders, and this is my partner, Detective Sergeant Eric Stone," he said as they showed their identification.

"Please, call me Jeannie. What can we do for you?" She noticed Stone was carrying a briefcase. Her gut told her the lake drive would have to wait. "By the way, this is Sean Delaney. He's with Interpol."

"Interpol? In almost twenty-one years in law enforcement, I've never run into an Interpol agent, in Idaho no less," Elders said, shaking Sean's hand. Jeannie felt that Elders appeared to have a snarky attitude. Perhaps he thought Sean, being an Interpol agent, would be a little uppity, especially with his British accent. However, Stone did not seem to have any animosity toward Sean and gave him a strong handshake.

"Would you mind if I used your table?" Stone asked, looking at the table and lifting his briefcase.

"I'm sorry. Please go ahead," Jeannie answered.

The four walked to the table and sat down. "Would you gentlemen like a cup of coffee or tea?" Sean asked. Jeannie doubted that either of the two law enforcement officers had ever been offered tea, much less by a British Interpol agent. The officers declined, but Jeannie said she would love a second cup.

Wearing a light brown suit and matching tie, his hair cut very short, and his face sporting a well-trimmed mustache, Sergeant Elders looked like a drill sergeant. Stone wore a blue suit with a black shirt and no tie. His hair was much longer than Elder's and styled in a comb-over, but he showed no sign of male pattern baldness. Clean-shaven, he looked younger than his partner and reeked of cigarettes, a habit confirmed by nicotine-yellowed fingers.

Detective Stone's youthful appearance made it obvious he was junior to Elders. Jeannie thought he was in his early thirties. *Must be a pretty good cop to make it to the rank of detective already,* she thought. Judging from his build, it was obvious he worked out with weights.

"Agent Loomis, I want to apologize for interrupting your vacation up here," Stone said as he placed the briefcase on the table and began pushing both clasps, but did not open it.

"Again, call me Jeannie."

"Who owns the Corvette outside? Elders asked, looking at Sean.

Maybe that's why he's a little cold with Delaney, Jeannie thought. "It's mine, and before you start questioning how an FBI agent can afford such a car, I used part of my inheritance," Jeannie said with a smile, looking at both detectives. There was a brief period of awkward silence.

"OK, Jeannie," Stone said as he looked angrily at his partner. He opened the case, and Jeannie saw several files. *Yep,* she thought. *Kiss the vacation goodbye.* An air of tense anticipation filled the room. "A few days ago, two of our off-duty patrol officers were elk hunting in an area called No Return Wilderness. Its full name is Frank Church-River of No Return Wilderness. It's a dense forest, and people go missing there every year. Most are solo hikers who get confused with the terrain and never make it back to their base camp. Others are hunters who take a fall and die of exposure, especially in the wintertime. Entering this area is like going back in time. Some of our best search-and-rescue teams have gotten confused there due to the many switchbacks, ravines, and mountain ranges.

"As I said, two of our officers, who are familiar with the area, set out to bag an elk when one of them tripped over this." From the first folder, he pulled out a colored picture of a human skull partially buried in soil. "They called us in, and we sent our forensic evidence team; they got there late afternoon the next day. There's no way to get there other than flying in. There are no roads, just big game trails. The forestry department keeps one area cleared for plane and helicopter access. Hunters, like our two officers, are flown in and dropped off. A professional hiker would know the area quite well. If we'd had our normal winter, there'd have been a ton of snow on the ground, and it would've taken them several days at best to get there. When the evidence team arrived, they began searching the immediate area, and, as you've probably guessed, they found more human remains."

"How many?" Jeannie asked as Stone pulled out the remaining files.

"To date, we've found three bodies, all female. The coroner says they're all Caucasian and about the same age. Obviously, it's someone's killing grounds."

"The medical examiner said the killer used Frangible rounds on the victims. They burst upon impact for maximum effect. He found bullet fragments embedded inside the skulls." Elders added.

"The evidence team called in our search and rescue and expanded their search radius, but they only found the three."

"Has your coroner estimated how long they've been out there?"

"The skull the officers discovered has been up there for about six years. The other two, for about four."

Jeannie was already lost in thought. *The killer or killers had to lure the victims to this particular area. I don't think he would have killed them somewhere and then moved the bodies here. No, I'm thinking this asshole is hunting his prey. This is his killing zone.*

"Jeannie, again, we're sorry for disturbing you and Agent Delaney while you're on vacation," Detective Stone said, almost also apologizing for the way his partner was acting. "We sent what we have to the BAU in Quantico, but there's a backlog due to that Covid bullshit. Our director attempted to contact your SAC Lomax since you have a reputation for successfully handling serial murder cases. We were told he was unavailable, and a secretary transferred him to an Agent Ismail Flores, whom we understand is taking your place while you're on vacation. He said one of the FBI's best behavioralists was right here in our backyard, so to speak. He even helped by giving us your cabin's address.

"I'll kill him when I get back to San Francisco," Jeannie said, smiling. "Tell you what, guys. Sean and I were about to take a cruise around the lake. Can you leave me your files, and when we get back, probably tomorrow, I'll give them a thorough examination and give you my input? We'll be up here for about a week. Will that work for you?"

The officers thanked Jeannie for her assistance in the case and recommended a few great restaurants to consider as they made their way around the lake, although Elders still seemed a little cool. They shook hands, and before they left, Jeannie gave them her cellphone number. She knew in her soul that this case already intrigued her. Another serial killer had been operating undetected for several years. He needed to be stopped, and if she could, she would help make that happen.

She recalled a recent investigation in Calistoga where a serial killer operated freely, unconcerned about being caught. This case was a lot different. Maybe that was why she wanted to drop everything and give it her full attention. A cunning predator was hunting defenseless prey!

Chapter Three

"OKAY, PEOPLE. TODAY is Sunday, February 7th, and, as you can see, the NFL Championship game is in progress. Millions of people worldwide are watching this modern-day gladiatorial battle, and today, we are about to give a lot of people a major heart attack. God, don't you just love it? We will wait until nine minutes after the halftime show so everyone will be back in their seats at the stadium or at home. The halftime shows have apparently been pretty bad these last few years, and people use that time to go to the bathroom or fill up their plates.

"In 1977, way before any of us were born, a movie was released called *Black Sunday*. With approximately 80,000 fans in attendance, along with the President of the United States, a terrorist group called Black September planned to fly the Goodyear blimp into the stadium to set off a device that would send shrapnel into the audience, killing thousands. It was a good movie, but not realistic.

"No, today, we will not use such a primitive method. Instead, we will use modern technology to shock the world, even if it is just for a few minutes and for our amusement. With the shutdown of the power grid blacking out the whole stadium and surrounding area, the world will get a taste of our power, a show of power, if you will. Also, tomorrow, more than 20,000 websites will simultaneously crash. FedEx, Amazon, HBO, Max, Call of Duty, Delta, McDonald's, and on and on—all will be impacted. That is when they will hear the name *Black Cell* for the first time.

"Much of the Internet will stop working due to the major outages we will cause across different apps and websites, including airlines, banks, and streaming services. People across the globe will not be able to tweet. So sad," he said while mocking the wiping away of a fake tear.

Akio Tanaka, a thirty-two-year-old computer genius listed on the NSA watchlist as the most dangerous hacker on the planet, was walking on air as he watched his team of hackers diligently monitor their computer screens while working their keyboards. Dressed in his preferred black short-sleeved t-shirt and Docker pants, he glanced at his second-in-charge, Yuma Masuta, a twenty-one-year-old Japanese female.

Slightly overweight with a poor complexion, she would not be noticed in a crowd. She wore a pair of white satin sweatpants and a matching top so sheer you could see her black lace bra beneath. Her long raven hair nearly reached her waist and shimmered when she walked under the few overhead lights.

"Now, we all know that once we cause these sites to crash tomorrow, a few minutes after our little show, these companies will reach out to their legal departments to prepare data breach response plans, including how notifications will flow internally and will include outside counsel and other vendors in the immediate aftermath of the incident. They will be in for a rude awakening when we shut down their lines of communication. It will be great!" he said with a laugh as he slid his right hand through his hair.

"These dumb shits will sit around their highly polished oak or mahogany conference tables waiting for a ransom call to come in. We will let them squirm for a few hours until I get bored, and then we will send them a happy face signed, *The Black Cell.* Sounds like they are getting ready to start the halftime entertainment." An announcer could be heard in the background introducing the first act.

Tanaka turned toward the large hanging television set showing the game. "Look at all those idiots who paid outrageous ticket prices with their hard-earned money to watch a bunch of overpaid jocks bang into each other. Not to forget the outlandish prices they are willing to pay for a hotdog, beer, and parking. The football commissioner is laughing all the way to the bank. Like little sheep, they wear the overpriced jerseys of their favorite teams while the league makes them feel guilty and has them stand for the Black National Anthem. What kind of shit is that?

"OK, get ready. Remember, our moment will come once we get into the third quarter."

***

Sean could tell by Jeannie's demeanor that her thoughts were on the serial killer case. She would start to describe a location as they passed, then stop mid-sentence, only to ask a bit later where she had left off. They spotted a restaurant one of the state police officers had mentioned and decided to stop.

Upon entering the main dining area, Jeannie realized it was Superbowl Sunday when she spotted several televisions in the bar area carrying the game. "Oh! I forgot, it's the Superbowl today. Looks like they're in the third quarter already," she said, not expecting a response from Sean.

"Did you want to get a room so you can watch it? We can always order room service."

"No, don't be silly. You only want to jump my bones again. I stopped watching football when that whole Kaepernick and BLM crap started. My dad and I were huge 49er and Steeler fans, but once the NFL allowed politics to enter their entertainment world, we stopped watching. I mean, gee, we now have a Black National Anthem?"

"Yes, in jolly old England, we can't understand why some Americans are upset over your former president wanting to see America First. I personally think a few people fantasize about a make-believe world they've seen on the screen while watching Star Trek. I'm surprised some of them aren't hoping for a spaceship to arrive as it did in *The Day the Earth Stood Still*, where robots controlled the inhabitants, not world governments."

"Don't worry. There're probably some of those people among us," Jeannie said, looking more closely at the menu.

Their attention was interrupted when they heard a television announcer suddenly say, "Sorry, folks. It appears we're having a power outage....." Then, the screen went black.

"Huh! Something like that happened during the last Super Bowl the Niners were in," Jeannie remarked.

"What do you mean?" Sean asked.

"I forget what quarter it was, but the players were on the field, and the lights started to flicker, and many went out. The officials had to postpone the game a little while for the players' and fans' safety. You'd think that after that embarrassment, the NFL would have made sure it never happened again. Especially during their biggest game of the year."

As they returned their attention to the menus, restaurant personnel tried other channels, but they were black as well. "What looks good to you?" Jeannie asked.

"Everything. To be honest, no matter what I select from an American menu, it always surprises me."

"In what way?"

"The portion sizes are enormous compared to Europe. I had a colleague who worked out of our Rome office. He and his wife were on holiday and visited me while in San Francisco. I took them to a nice Italian restaurant since they wanted to compare real Italian food with what was available here in the States. Anyway, both were astounded when their meals came. The wife asked if this was a family serving that we were supposed to share. When I said no, that the heaped pile of spaghetti on her plate was all hers, she made the sign of the cross and muttered that this could be the cause of obesity in the U.S."

Jeannie appeared to be listening but wasn't, at least not actively. Sean felt there was a little too much silence. *Is Jeannie already attempting to solve her new investigation? Is this what life would be like if we moved on in our relationship?*

Before they could order, Sean's cellphone began to vibrate. "Headquarters," he said, looking at Jeannie. "Yes, sir. I can hear you. I understand. Right, I'll jump on it immediately. Yes, once I arrive and get things set up, I'll contact you."

"Bad?" Jeannie asked.

"Very bloody bad!"

Chapter Four

THEY DECIDED THAT Jeannie should drive back to her cabin while Sean made phone calls. Apparently, the blackout was not a simple circuit breaker or two malfunctioning but an external intruder who had shut down the entire power grid in the area where the championship game was being held. Simultaneously, mainstream media feeds were also shut down, and their internal power was cut off. The blackout was still going when Jeannie and Sean reached the cabin, a span of over ninety minutes.

From what Jeannie overheard, the responsible party had somehow hacked into the power system of the network covering the Super Bowl. When the network tried to switch over to auxiliary power, they found it had also been compromised. Sean was on a roll, and she was impressed with how quickly he was formulating a plan of action. *That's my boy,* she thought.

"I'm afraid the higher-ups are going to cut my holiday with you short. I do apologize." Jeannie felt that Sean was genuinely disappointed about not being able to spend time with her at the cabin. *Maybe it was just the sex he'd miss out on, but who knew.* "What do you Yanks say? Can I get a rain check?"

"Absolutely. And hey, when things get tough, Interpol wants their best man. I guess I'll just have to get used to it. Anything you can share?"

"As far as we can tell, your NSA received a communiqué from a group calling themselves the Black Cell. The email didn't explain their motivation. I'm afraid it'll be left up to various law enforcement communities to discover that, but somehow, they were able to hack into the network feeds carrying the football game worldwide."

"How does that involve Interpol?"

"I asked that, and after getting my ass chewed, I was told that preliminary tracking shows the intruders were operating near Kyiv, Ukraine. It's been my experience in cases like this that these people are long gone, and their tracks are already well concealed."

"Yes, our intelligence sources indicate that most sophisticated hackers operate out of Eastern Europe, you know, Russia, Ukraine, and, of course, don't forget China."

"I'm afraid you're right, and that's why Interpol's been asked to get involved in the investigation. To be honest with you, anytime we have to deal with these nefarious countries, our chances of getting cooperation are slim to none. If these people would use their talents in non-criminal ways, think of the money they'd make working for high-tech firms. Of course, then you and I would be out of a job."

***

"That was great," Tanaka said to his Black Cell hackers. "The Internet is lit up with stories about our hacks. Unfortunately, there were some deaths and injuries. Several fell in the dark and were hurt in the stadium. There were also numerous traffic accidents, and some of the hospitals realized, too late, that their backup generators would not work. But you cannot have victory without some collateral damage. As they say, practice makes perfect, and we have only just begun. Now, we need to hurry down the rabbit hole while our pursuers attempt to locate our base of operation. If you have any problems, check with Yuma. There is no time to waste. In several days, we will cause more havoc."

***

Jeannie and Sean had little time for small talk. Sean was busy answering and returning calls. Fortunately, a sizeable snow front held off until they reached the airport. Before Sean got out of the car, he reached over and pulled Jeannie as far as he could toward him and gave her a long passionate kiss. "I'm so sorry to cut this magnificent holiday with you short. I believe this won't be an easy case to pursue, but I promise to call you whenever I can."

"You'd better!"

Jeannie got out and popped the sportscar's small trunk hatch open and waited for Sean to remove his suitcase and briefcase. Setting them on the ground, he gave her another long embrace and kiss.

"Have a safe flight. Call me when you arrive in France."

"For sure, and next time we'll fly to France together." He waved as he approached the terminal entrance.

Catching a tear falling from her right eye, Jeannie got back into the driver's seat and started for home. The snow was becoming heavy, but Jeannie didn't care. The road was still maneuverable for the Corvette, although if a thick layer of snow started to accumulate, it could be problematic. She was lost in thought. *Sean seemed a little different at dinner. It's like he's keeping something from me.*

Her thoughts then jumped to the Super Bowl hackers and the unknown serial killer who had been hunting his prey for too long without being caught.

She surmised that the hackers' true motivations had not been revealed. *Probably another Goldfinger who wants total world domination. They have to be intelligent to pull off what they've done so far, and accomplishing that from overseas is no small feat.*

Now, the serial killer, I'm just going to speculate here. But I believe he's a male, a hunter, and a person who really knows that area. What I don't know yet, is how he seduces his victims. Going to be interesting!

***

Despite several layovers and flight changes to Lyons, France, the flight was tolerable. Sean thought about Jeannie and again had some doubts about a long-term relationship with her. He really liked her, but both were so committed to their jobs that red flags were waving. He never told her about his real job at Interpol, a life filled with international travel and intrigue. Ismail had been right when he teased Jeannie about her new lover being a modern-day James Bond. More doubts flooded his thoughts about the two of them. It was unfair to Jeannie, and he soon had to decide what to do.

With no babies nearby to keep him awake, his thoughts drifted to what the motivation might be for the hacking job and who made up the Black Cell. He mulled over the small note they had sent to the NSA that had, in turn, been forwarded to him.

> "For too long, the inhabitants of this planet have accepted corruption in politics and allowed the so-called elite to make all the world's decisions. Those occupying these high-level positions, when caught, are not held to the same standards as the average person. No, instead, they are surrounded by their corrupt compatriots who put a 'spin' on their criminal enterprises, allowing them to escape with no accountability. Tonight, you witnessed just a little of the awesome power of the Black Cell. In a few days, you will see phase two. Have a nice day."

Wish I had received this sooner, Sean thought. *Jeannie might have been able to give me the author's psychological profile.* He had read and re-read the communiqué and could only think of a few possibilities. Obviously, the author considered himself, or herself, both judge and executioner. To pull off such a feat, they had to be highly intelligent, organized, and well-financed. He had handled only a few computer crimes in his career, and it was mostly a case of tracking down the location of the source and apprehending the suspect, who was usually a loner. Others were related to child pornography and wire fraud, but the Black Cell case was unusual and very different.

As he had assumed, the intelligence gathered by the NSA and CIA showed the group operated behind numerous firewalls, dummies, and shell corporations, so much so that the exact location of the operation would be very difficult to find. To be able to hack halfway across the planet was no small feat. *Well, maybe it isn't. With modern technology, maybe it's easy to do. What do I know about hacking?* He asked himself.

Chapter Five

SEAN'S SCENT LINGERED within her empty cabin. *Well, old girl. I think you're hooked on James Bond, aren't you? Sure, there are some small red flags, but what relationship doesn't have them?* She went upstairs and started to make the bed but then decided to cozy up on Sean's side and fell asleep, waking up about three hours later. *Well, hell! What am I going to do now?* She took a long shower and went downstairs. They had not had time to stock the refrigerator other than what they had brought for breakfast. Jeannie found one egg, a few hash browns, and a quarter link of linguiça. She caught herself smiling. *Wonder what Ismail's going to say when I tell him Sean loves his Portuguese sausage?*

She began to question her feelings for Sean. She was very attracted to him, but why? Was it simply his British accent and mannerisms? *No, I can't be that shallow. He's very handsome and treats me with respect, but we really haven't been together for long. That was the purpose of this getaway, to spend time together and get to know each other better. And what about those recent feelings of secrecy? Could it be me, since I don't exactly have a good track record with long-term relationships, much less marriage? Slow down, girl! Who's talking about marriage?*

Hell, maybe it's me being a little too pushy and forward with Sean. What do I really know about the man? He works with Interpol. We worked together on the Ark investigation, and then, after one dinner, I started wanting more. Maybe that's why I'm starting to feel a little weird.

Finishing her second cup of tea, she called Ismail. Once again, he had been appointed as Jeannie's replacement at the San Francisco Bureau of Investigation. "Hey, Ace. How's it going? I hope you haven't destroyed my office. You know, I am coming back."

"Hey, boss lady. How goes the romantic getaway with 007?"

"Cut short, I'm afraid. Sean was called back since Interpol has been called in on the Super Bowl hacking. Are we involved?"

"Nah. I think that since the game was played on the east coast, we'll escape the investigation unless things point here. Sorry to hear that your squeeze was called away. Anything else exciting going on?" he asked with a hint of a laugh as if he already knew the answer.

"As a matter of fact, yes, there is. Thanks to you. Remember what they say, payback is a bitch."

"Hey, what was I supposed to say when the Idaho State Police called me? I mean, here's one of the foremost authorities on serial killers in their backyard. They needed help in the worst way, and I couldn't withhold your availability to a fellow law enforcement agency."

"Very funny. But, that said, at least I won't be bored up here. It's an interesting case from what I've learned so far. Two off-duty officers go out elk hunting and stumble on human remains. Next thing they know, they find the killer's hunting ground."

"How do you know it's not just a body drop?"

"I think he's hunting his prey in the wilderness area. He transports them there and then plays his deadly game. I really haven't dived into their files yet. I'd hoped to wait until sometime this week, but with Sean now gone, what the hell. So, how's it going down there? Oh, by the way, you got Sean hooked on linguiça."

"Hey, what can I say. The Brits have nothing to compare with my Portuguese linguiça. Now, the Poles, they have blood sausage, that's like our morcela, but I'm not sure 007 would like it. I'll suggest it the next time I see him."

***

Senator Jill Fisher had her sights set on the big ring, the presidency. As chairperson of the Democratic Party, she felt well placed for consideration since the sitting president was in no shape to run for a second term, neither physically nor mentally. Yes, she was almost seventy-three years old, but her plastic surgeons had done a masterful job of making her appear to be in her late sixties. *Nothing like a boob job, cheek implants, butt lift, and a few facelifts to fool the public,* she thought.

She climbed out of her sunken bathtub and put on her Versace Baroque bathrobe, allowing it to dry her off. Sitting at her dresser and beginning to brush her hair, she gazed into the mirror and studied her face. *More damned crow's feet. Need to see Dr. Rathbun again.* She reached over and grabbed her laptop. *Time to check on my investments.*

Frustration coursed through her veins as she entered a wrong passcode and had to repeat the process. She hated it when various offshore banks wanted her to change her passwords so often. What really irked her was when she tried to use a new password and was informed she had used it in the past and needed a different one.

She finally got in but immediately thought she had done something wrong when she saw a zero balance. *That can't be right,* she thought out loud to herself. *There should be at least $800,000 in that one account alone.* She made a mental note to contact the bank and give them a piece of her mind.

She found it easier to access her bank account in the Cayman Islands but was shocked to find that account also showing a zero balance. "What the fuck is going on?" she shouted to an empty bedroom. She knew she was the only one with the passwords to these accounts. She tried her largest account and again found a zero balance. Panicking, she felt her heart race. What could she do? She couldn't contact law enforcement; that would expose her money-laundering scheme with the Mexican drug cartel. Her heart was now pounding, trying to thump out of her chest. Gasping, she took her last breath. There would be no run for the presidency. Black Cell's second phase had claimed its first victim!

Early morning at the NSA headquarters

"OK, people. Everyone should have a copy of the email sent by this Black Cell. What do we have thus far?" Asked Assistant NSA Director Paul Falconer, a sixty-two-year-old who had made it to the top the old-fashioned way: he earned it. His glare could strike fear into any man's heart. He could level anyone with one look, and the recipient would immediately know to shut the fuck up. His surprisingly blush-red face, probably caused by high blood pressure agitated by working in a highly political agency led by a new administration, made him appear to be permanently sweating. Dressed in black slacks and pale-blue polo shirt and sporting a shaved head that seemed to glow when he walked under an overhead light, he barked out commands while repeatedly repositioning his glasses up to the bridge of his nose.

Agent Jamie Pierson was the first to speak up. Tall and big-boned, the twenty-five-year-old was known as an ass kisser by many of his fellow co-workers. He frequently wore a shirt with the M.I.T. logo, so everyone was reminded he was an alumnus, and in conversations, he often found a way to interject that he graduated at the top of his class. "Sir, as expected, the commands for the hack came from this area," he began, using a laser pointer to circle an area on the map east of Kyiv, the main Ukrainian city. "These apartments are for low-income individuals. Ground agents spoke to several people who confirmed that between ten and twelve individuals occupied this particular unit for six days, quickly leaving last night or early this morning. We're attempting to lift prints from the complex, but so far, we only know that the group was made up of both males and females, and apparently of different races."

"OK. That's a start. What else?"

"The group, Black Cell, was very good at erasing its signature during the hacks," said Tim Goldstein, a white male with a waist-length ponytail. "We have slides that show all the various hubs the group bounced their commands through. We focused on one, and that directed us to another, and so on. We went through fifty hubs before we were finally able to pin it down to that one apartment. This wasn't the work of amateur hackers."

"What can we do to track them down from here?" Falconer asked. No one responded. "Anyone? We need to do better. This is a major priority, so get back to work."

***

On the surface, most Interpol jobs entail paper chases. When Sean read about jurisdictions and the types of crimes Interpol investigates, he chuckled about the part they are supposed to play in rooting out political corruption. *Hell, that alone would tie down an organization for a century,* he thought.

Sean was part of a secret branch of Interpol that very few were privy to, a branch that his new friend, Ismail Flores, would easily recognize as a spy world. *Yes, Ismail, my dear friend, you don't know how close you were when you jokingly referred to me as Mr. Bond, James Bond.*

With a total budget just south of $200,000,000, a small amount was dedicated to this special branch, hidden in accounting records and never to be listed. Even Sean was unaware of exactly how many special agents belonged to his clandestine unit. Their covert activities were only known to a select few. Following the loss of Sean's wife to cancer, Interpol felt it prudent to transfer him to a desk job at the San Francisco branch office.

Fortunately, he met Jeannie. He was lonely and felt the need for female companionship, but he knew this was something he should have avoided. He felt selfish and knew that, eventually, he would hurt her. He should never have allowed himself to bring Jeannie into his world where he could never share the secretive side of his Interpol position with her.

When Sean entered a large room occupied by his counterparts, Secretary-General Jurgen Stock stood, stared at him, and waited for him to find a seat. Sean's footsteps echoed through the large room. To call Stock overbearing and imposing would be an understatement; he was not someone you would want to cross. Many Interpol agents had their careers abruptly ended after locking horns with him. There was a palpable tension in the room. Even a slight noise reverberated off the walls. Sean thought of one of the many Bond films where a famous spy enters a large meeting room with all eyes upon him.

Wearing a three-piece blue suit with a lighter blue tie, Stock began his presentation. "Now we're all here, we can start. As you're aware, the Americans had their Super Bowl game disrupted this Sunday." Behind him was a large globe map projected onto an enormous screen secured at the ceiling. "After an approximately ninety-two-minute blackout, an email was delivered to the United States National Security

Agency, the NSA. Each of you has been provided with a copy of the email." Several glanced at their cellphone email display.

"Those responsible call themselves the Black Cell. Catchy phrase, although we don't know what it means. Suffice it to say, they're very good at what they do. Reaching out from Ukraine, they traversed almost halfway around the world and took out most television networks. While we were summoning each of you here, we were in contact with other intelligence and police agencies to identify, locate, and stop this group from their threatened next attack, whatever and whenever that may be.

"Each of you will find your assignment in the packet you've received. If you have questions, see me. That's it, gentlemen. I believe this is only the tip of the iceberg. Let me stress that this is a serious international problem."

Delaney broke the seal around his packet, opened it, and found a photograph of a young Asian female. Turning it over, he saw her listed name as Yuma Masuta, twenty-one years old, 5'5", and 155 lbs. Her last known address was her parents' home in Osaka, Japan. *Wouldn't be bad looking if she lost some weight, but man, there's something sinister about her persona. Is this the leader of the Black Cell? I've never heard of an all-female hacker gang, but in the spirit of equality, why not?* As he was looking through the rest of his packet, a female approached. "Agent Delaney, the director would like a word with you." She was very businesslike in her delivery.

He followed her down two hallways, and upon reaching a closed door, she knocked, turned, and walked away. "Come in." Delaney entered to see both the director and deputy director sitting at a table. "Delaney, so good you could make it. Sorry to spoil your holiday. How are you getting along? How does the San Francisco weather fare with you?"

Delaney knew the director and deputy director could not give a rat's ass about his answers, so he simply answered, "Fine, sir." Both the director and deputy director were upper-crust bureaucrats, and they liked their booze. There had been rumors that the deputy director was gay. The director was extremely overweight, and his mustache gave him the appearance of a walrus. He seemed to always have a pipe in his mouth or hand; sometimes filled with tobacco, sometimes not.

"Good, good. Glad to hear it. Please, take a seat. Delaney, as you have no doubt seen in your dossier, you will be going to Japan to learn as much as you can about Ms. Masuta."

"What makes her so special to the investigation, if I might ask, sir?"

"I'd be surprised if you didn't. Thomas, you want to address that?"

The deputy director was not as imposing as the director; in fact, he was very meek until he started to drink. He had a thin build with a full head of hair that needed some form of management. Sean envisioned him as a troll doll with a wild hairdo. He folded his hands in front of him and leaned forward against the table. "When the American football game was blacked out, Japanese law enforcement quickly informed us that they had rudimentary information on a group calling themselves the Black Cell, and this young lady is apparently involved. To what extent, they don't know.

"Don't let her looks deceive you, Delaney. She's a lethal combination of brains, ambition, and fanaticism. Her IQ is off the charts according to Japanese intelligence, and her prowess with computers is second to none.

"Yama Masuta is a stone-cold serial killer. Most people believe that serial killers are male, yet female serial killers have accounted for just over eleven percent of all cases in the past century. In more recent decades, it's between five and seven percent. Their prevalence is also far more stable, with only a few dozen operating in any given decade."

"Yama is one of them," the director said, cutting the deputy director off. "Most like to use poison, but not her. No, she delights in administering extreme torture, prolonging death for as long as she can. She would slice your balls off while you're asleep, then roll over in your blood and go back to sleep.

"Masuta's father was a member of Yakuza and a high-ranking member, I might add.

In modern-day Japan, the Yakuza extort, smuggle, blackmail, run prostitution rings, engage in drug trafficking, do human smuggling, run restaurants and bars, and run many other businesses. Within the gang's hierarchy, their assassins occupy a high level.

"They're heavily tattooed, a tradition going back to the samurai. The more tattoos, the more respect a Yakuza receives. Of course, they hide them from the public. Today, sporty business suits cover them up. They're viewed by many as modern-day Robin Hoods, something like the people of Chicago and their love for Al Capone. They look at them as a noble, divine group, much like the samurai. They're seen as gangs that protect and assure survival by using both legal and illegal means, rather than simply going out and hurting people, and they are often glorified with dignity and, in a sense, justice."

The deputy director took over. "Yuma's father was a throw-back to an earlier time. A time when a Yakuza member took pride in having others watch them endure the pain of being tattooed, especially on the most sensitive parts of the body. We have documentation that her father executed over 42 people in the most violent of ways. In one case, he skinned a person alive. This is the DNA that created Yuma. She wanted to join the Yakuza, which was impossible, even with her father holding his high-ranking position. So, she started her own female Yakuza gang.

"Her father died about seven years ago. It's believed this was when she left her mother, but we're not sure.

Not much is known about her mother. Rumors suggest she was nothing more than a Yakuza groupie. She became pregnant, and instead of dumping her, Yuma's father married her, obeying a code of respect and honor.

"Delaney, if Yuma's involved in this Black Cell hacking operation, she'll have to be eliminated. She won't go quietly, as they say in American films. Whether she's the brains behind the operation or on the fringe, be careful. She's a killer like no one in our organization has seen before."

Delaney began considering what may have motivated the Black Cell's recent hack job and threats of more to come. The Super Bowl blackout was just the beginning, an act to draw attention to the group. Why? He did not know. He blocked out the two directors' mundane conversation. "Delaney?"

"Yes, sir. Sorry, I was thinking about the Black Cell's motivation."

"Once again, we're going after a person or group of sociopaths who have no real attachment to anyone and see others as objects. The leader of the group probably fosters feelings of inner rage and uses it to justify negative behavior. Whoever it is undoubtedly has a sense of entitlement and seeks notoriety and money and power to control others. In other words, another nut job with delusional fantasies of wealth, power, or omnipotence having visions of grandiose or extravagant things or actions, like the Super Bowl blackout.

This should be fun, Sean thought to himself.

Chapter Six

"HELLO, JEANNIE. HOW are you?" were the first words out of Sean's mouth when Jeannie answered her cell.

"I'm great now. Where are you, or can't you say?" an excited Jeannie replied.

"Right now, I'm at the Lyon-Saint Exupery Airport, ready to catch a plane to Japan."

"Japan? That's where the investigation's taking you?"

"Fraid so. Duty calls and all that stuff."

Jeannie laughed. "I miss you. The cabin's not the same without you."

"I miss you terribly also. How's the serial killer case going? Have you been officially assigned, or are you still operating as a consultant?"

"Still a consultant. Actually, I just came back from the store. I bought a whiteboard and markers. You'd be proud of me. I hung it up all by myself."

"Of course, you did. You're a highly trained FBI agent!"

"You sound like Ismail. Anyway, I was just listing the case's known points. I feel he's hunting his victims. I've already listed some areas that need to be examined more closely."

"I pity that poor chap. He doesn't know who he's up against. Oh, they're making the final call for boarding. It'll be a long flight, so I don't know when I'll be able to call again. Think of me, love. Bye." And with that, he was off.

Jeannie took a deep breath and suppressed a tear. If she were home in Newark, she could have at least shared her feelings with her koi. Instead, she went downstairs, grabbed the remains of a cold roast beef sandwich and a can of diet Dr. Pepper she had picked up at Subway, and went back upstairs to her study. She had drawn three columns on the whiteboard. Since no one had been identified yet, there were no photos to add. Each column was headed "Victim," and the number identified such as Victim #1, Victim #2, and Victim #3.

She noted similarities like appearance, hair length, and hair color. They were all blond or brunette, all Caucasian, 5'2" to 5'5", with average weight and build. None were close to being obese. *Huh,* she thought, *no common thread between them so far that could lead somewhere.*

She remembered another case she had worked on many years ago, where a serial killer kidnapped young elementary female students. He raped and tortured them before throwing their bodies down wells in the agricultural areas of Stockton, Manteca, and Tracy, California. On this unofficial consulting job in Idaho, she was feeling a similar sense of rage as she had then. The killer in California seemed to flaunt his ability to outsmart the police. As the noose tightened around him, he took the coward's way out and committed suicide. She had always felt an emptiness about that case. The killer never really faced justice. He never had to face a jury of his peers, a lifelong sentence in prison, or the hot shot. *This stupid state has the death penalty, but San Quentin Prison is full of murderers living at the taxpayers' expense.* Jeannie had not been able to inflict corporal punishment for what he had done. *I mean, one 9 mm round would only cost around $1.00.*

Jeannie gave the case another three hours and then decided to give it a break and leave it for the next day. She showered, shampooed her hair, and found that Sean had left his BLV Notte shower gel on the shower stall. She unscrewed the cap and was overwhelmed by Sean's distinctive aroma. After lathering up with his gel and showering for a second time, she felt better.

Engulfed in her thick terrycloth bathrobe, she turned on the master bedroom television and heard,

"....to date, a group identifying themselves as the Black Cell has taken credit for the Super Bowl hacking. Little is known about the group, as law enforcement is withholding information." *Of course they are, you liberal assholes. What do you want them to do? Give you all their information so you can hold a sit down with the suspects and get a jump on your rival news agencies? Give me a break,* she vented out loud. She switched channels and found a good "who-done-it" movie, *Certain Prey* with Mark Harmon, an adaption of John Sandford's Prey novel series. The movie was about a female hitwoman who eventually teams up with a criminal defense attorney who is also female. Together, they commit homicides, feeling they can outsmart the police.

Jeannie enjoyed watching and reading this genre, feeling that suspects might use similar materials and plots they find in books and movies to commit crimes. It helped her get into their heads and better understand their motivations and what made them tick.

Barely staying awake long enough to see the end of the movie, she turned off the television, said her prayers, and fell asleep. Even though she had slept in the cabin alone before, without Sean, the sounds emanating from the structure were eerier. She recalled her dad explaining to her when she was small and had nightmares that some houses are relatively quiet while others are downright talkative. Pops, bangs, or creaks in the dead of night can be startling, but, in most cases, these sounds are just a home's reaction to temperature changes.

Or maybe, it is the spirit of Frank Silva and his band of Banshees returning from their Ark of the Covenant theft. Just in case, she reached for her nightstand and found her Glock. *A girl has to be prepared. Isn't that what nosy neighbor Delores said the day she came over to show off her shooting ability by hitting a paper target?*

At 7:00 a.m., the sun invaded her sleep through an easterly facing window. She turned over and tried to avoid it, but it won out. Stretching, she could smell Sean's shower gel on both her pillows and sheets.

Not wanting to embarrass herself or anyone coming to her door that early in the morning while she was wearing nothing more than her bathrobe, she dressed before venturing downstairs to make herself a breakfast of toast, tea, scrambled eggs, linguiça, and fried potatoes. *Yep, that should hold me over until lunch.* She had just finished preparing her second cup of tea when her cell rang. She hoped it was Sean but was disappointed when the display showed it was the SAC, Lomax, her boss.

"Good morning. You're up bright and early," Jeannie answered.

"Hi, Jeannie. I wish this were a personal call, but it's formal. Now don't kill the messenger, okay?"

"What's up?" she said, feeling tightness in her chest.

"The Office of Professional Responsibility is investigating you and your actions in relation to the shooting death of Dr. Hausser and that whole Nazi investigation."

"But that was cleared by our own shooting team when they flew in right after the incident! What a bunch of crap! I smell Washington D.C. bullshit all over this. Is this retaliation for not kissing up to those damned sexist, white, corrupt male bureaucrats at the top of the bureau?"

"Jeannie. Are you through?"

"Sorry, sir. All these years busting my ass for the bureau, and now I'm being questioned by my own agency over the shooting of a suspect who shot me? I didn't even have a gun. What a bunch of crap."

"Look. I got mad as hell when they notified me, and I did a little digging among my contacts. Between you and me, you're correct; this is a bunch of bullshit. As you know, when we were investigating those involved with Dr. Hausser and his Fourth Reich, we became aware of how the modern-day Nazi movement has infiltrated major corporations and politics. Remember, they called themselves the Organization?

"Herr Doctor's killing pissed the Organization and their command structure off, and they want to show their followers they're not afraid of taking on the FBI, specifically, you. For whatever reason, they're not going after agent Delaney," Lomax explained.

"So, what do I do? I assume, by standard protocol, your call is to suspend me with pay, pending the outcome of the investigation, correct?"

"You know the drill. Paid suspension pending the investigation. Now, unfortunately, since this involves the State Department and Austria, it's going to take God knows how long to get resolved. If our guy were still in office, he would have told Austria to go to hell, but with what we have in the White House now, who knows how long it will take? Here's what I want you to do. The IA people will contact you shortly, and they'll want you to come in and surrender your weapon and give a statement. I know you'll want to tell them to go fuck themselves, but please, don't say that. Play the damn game. When you get through with them, let's go grab lunch or a late breakfast, depending on the time of day, OK? I know you'll contact Ismail, but only tell him the basics. You don't want to drag him into all this shit."

***

Congressman Emmet Carlson was a shining example of everything wrong in Congress. His net worth before being elected was around $72,000. After twenty-nine years in office, he was a multi-millionaire with three houses, a super yacht, and a private jet. He was another of the Washington elites who despised former President Trump for trying to drain the swamp that he loved to wallow in. There were no progressive demands that he did not sign up for. He did not see the irony of flying in his private jet, wasting thousands of taxpayers' dollars in jet fuel, to attend a "climate change" conference. Of course, he made sure to take advantage of any photo ops, making a few statements for the press and then returning to his suite for sexual escapades with high-priced call girls.

Carlson was a strong believer in, "you scratch my back, and I'll scratch yours." The drug and sex trades had always been good to him. He even got a taste of the profits from the infamous gun trafficking fiasco between 2006 and 2011. It was a sweet tactic used by the Arizona U.S. Attorney's Office and the Arizona Field Office of the United States Bureau of Alcohol, Tobacco, Firearms and Explosives, or the AFT, as it was known.

The scam involved a series of operations in the Tucson and Phoenix areas where the ATF deliberately allowed licensed firearms dealers to sell weapons to illegal straw buyers, hoping to track the guns to Mexican drug cartel leaders and arrest them. The intended result was to stem the flow of firearms into Mexico by interdicting straw purchasers and gun traffickers within the U.S.

It was a matter of Washington blundering, but no one really cared as long the money flowed into their coffers. The stated goal of allowing these purchases was to continue to track the firearms as they were transferred to higher-level drug traffickers and key figures in Mexican cartels, with the expectation this would lead to their arrests and dismantling.

While federal prosecutors told agents they had no choice but to let guns "walk" and ordered them not to arrest buyers, the tactic of allowing obvious straw purchasers to give guns to criminal organizations was questioned during the operations by ATF field agents and cooperating licensed gun dealers. A border patrol agent was killed with one of these weapons, and nothing was done to those who allowed it to happen.

During *Operation Fast and Furious*, the largest gun trafficking probe, the ATF monitored the sale of about 2,000 firearms, of which only 710 were recovered. A number of straw purchasers were arrested and indicted; however, all tracks leading to corrupt politicians were covered. Carlson netted a cool million.

Carlson entered his private den. It was an impressive room with floor-to-ceiling walnut bookcases encased in etched glass, each section independently illuminated to showcase first editions, which Carlson had no intention of reading. A sliding ladder to the right of the shelving made it possible for anyone interested to reach a book on the upper tiers. A globe aquarium containing several colorful saltwater fish sat on a stand in one corner.

The opposite wall was adorned with another custom-designed saltwater aquarium teeming with fish worth thousands of dollars. But money was no object; illegal bribes continued to trickle in. The walnut-paneled wall behind Carlson's desk hid a hidden compartment containing his safe filled with unreported money. The room reeked of smoke that became denser as Carlson lit another Cuban cigar and turned on his computer.

"This must be a mistake," he said out loud to himself. He re-entered his username and password, which again brought up one of his many offshore accounts. Balance: zero. "What the hell! A zero balance?" he yelled out to the empty room. Panicking, he logged in to all nine accounts. Each had a zero balance. The Black Cell was moving along with Phase Two.

Chapter Seven

DELANEY WAS MET with a fine mist as he left the confines of Osaka airport. Without an umbrella, he held his briefcase over his head to avoid messing up his hair while carrying his suitcase in his other hand. A taxi was waiting at the curb. Osaka is the capital and most populous city in Osaka Prefecture and the third most populous city in Japan, behind only Tokyo and Yokohama. The driver tried to be friendly and converse, but Sean apologized, saying he was beat from the long flight and had numerous text messages to address.

Interpol had a room reserved for him at the Marriott Miyako Hotel. At $289 per night, Sean was impressed with his surroundings. Of course, this fit into his cover, that of a highly successful businessman associated with a high-tech startup company in the U.S.

Physically and mentally drained, he called room service and ordered tuna sushi and tea. He thought about sake but decided against it. Once finished with his meal, he took a hot shower instead of planning his agenda. He would put that off until the morning when he had more energy. It was hard for him to stay asleep, a problem he often had when sleeping in a strange bed. At 6:00 a.m., he was wide awake and decided to visit the hotel's gym and then sit a spell in the hot tub to relieve tension in his back.

His thoughts turned to Jeannie, and he began feeling guilty about leading her on. He really liked and cared for her but had vacillating feelings that he tried to stop, but it was hard. When he was charmed by her voice, he said what he thought she wanted to hear, and that was unfair.

Refreshed and shaved, he put on one of his designer suits and visited the hotel's restaurant for a continental breakfast. A few other Caucasians were present, but most people were of Japanese descent. Finishing breakfast and leaving a generous tip, he stopped at reception and asked if he had received any messages. He knew there would be a package waiting for him.

"No messages, Mr. Delaney, but you do have a package."

He tipped the young male receptionist, placed the box under his arm, and walked to the bank of elevators. Once in his room, he placed the package on his unmade bed and opened it. As expected, he found a Ruger .22 Long pistol with a suppressor. The

Japanese Interpol office had dropped the weapon off earlier. *This will do quite nicely,* he said to himself.

Delaney had always loved Japan. He had been there on assignments several times and found the culture an interesting blend of Eastern traditions and Western modernity that was evident throughout the country. Outside its major cities, the country is home to some of the best and most natural scenery in the world. He was particularly fond of their great sushi.

On the road, he passed several koi farms that reminded him of Jeannie and her koi fish aquarium in her Newark home. *Bet she would love seeing this. Note to self, bring Jeannie to koi farms in Japan.* Driving a rental car was not a problem for Delaney. The Japanese drive on the left of the road as they do in England.

The car's GPS said he had almost reached his destination: Yuma Masuta's mother's home, Yuma's last known address. It was in the poorer section of the city with high-density housing. With land at a premium, there were many high-rise tenements constructed of cheap building materials. Each unit seemed to have the daily clothes washing on display, drying in the breeze. Yakuza is embedded here, he thought.

Sean drove past the house and found a roadside coffee shop just down the street. From there, he would observe the goings and comings at the residence. An hour and two cups of tea later, he was bored and in need of a bathroom. *Nothing will happen while I'm in the loo,* he hoped.

When he returned, a red Sakuta motor scooter pulled to the curb directly in front of his table. A female rider got off the scooter, removed her helmet, shook her hair loose, and revealed a very athletic face that matched her athletic body. About 5'2" in height, she was wearing black leather pants and a leather vest over a blue long-sleeved pullover sweatshirt. She looked at him, smiled, and waved. This elicited an automatic wave in return. She placed the helmet on the bike seat and, pulling her raven black hair into a ponytail, walked over to Sean.

Thinking his cover was blown and a sympathizer of Yakusa was approaching, he instinctively patted his right chest area, feeling the security of his gun in its shoulder holster. "Relax, agent Delaney. I'm a friend, not a foe." With a beautiful smile, she walked closer to him and extended her hand. Sean shook it. Showing him her credentials, she said, "I am Akari from the Tokyo branch. I know you are probably tired of tea, but I need one. Perhaps we can take a walk after I get some?"

Sean checked the surroundings and did not see anything amiss. "That would be delightful," he said as he pushed his chair closer to the table and waited for her return. As she was walking back, he left the magazine on the table to free his hands.

"Ready?" she asked as she began walking to the exit. She smelled like freshly cut carnations, and when she spoke, her voice was youthful.

"I hope you don't think me rude, but how old are you, exactly?"

"I am old enough to have been an Interpol agent here for seven years," she said, suppressing a laugh. "But, if you must know, I am twenty-nine, well, thirty in ten days. I won't ask your age since I have already been briefed on you."

"I hope the information is accurate."

"Let's see. Sean Delaney. Sorry, Agent Sean Delaney. Special Branch. Forty-two years old. Born in Liverpool. That's where the Beatles came from, yes?" Not waiting for an answer, she continued. "Mother died during childbirth. Natural father turned to drink, no doubt due to the trauma of losing your mother. He died in a car crash. It is believed he was intoxicated at the time, but by then, you had already enlisted in the Royal Air Force. There, you excelled in your training. In fact, many of your feats in Special Forces training still stand as high-water marks that other recruits aim for. Your current assignment is branch director at our San Francisco office. I'm sure that is just a cover. I wish I could elaborate more, but you are actually a ghost. Most of your career is classified. How did I do?"

"You left out my shoe size and the type of toothpaste I use."

"Right. I will put that on my list of future research to be conducted later. Shall we sit for a spell?"

"Please." As Delaney began to sit, he continued to survey their surroundings. Akari noticed.

"Your presence has been noted by individuals associated with Yakuza ever since you arrived. There is a heavy presence of the gang here, as you probably suspected. What did you expect with this being Yuma's birthplace and the territory her father used to control before his death? I have been watching you and thought you were about to make a move on the house. You would have never been seen again. No offense."

"None taken. Were you sent here to spy on me or for another purpose?" Delaney asked.

"Let's take your car back to your hotel, and I will explain everything over an early dinner."

"What about your scooter?"

"Leave it. Someone will steal it within the hour."

They got to Sean's car, and the vehicle immediately took on the scent of carnations. "I love the perfume you're wearing."

"Flattery will get you everywhere, Agent Delaney.

"Please, call me Sean."

"OK. Sean it is. It is a brand carried by the American chain store Victoria's Secret. It is called Peaches and Cream. I am glad you like it."

"That's what it smells like. For some reason, I thought carnations, but no, it is peaches I smell. So, you have been with the agency for seven years. Have they all been in Japan?"

"Yes. I have put in for many transfers, but they have all been denied. The reasons given are always the same. You are a valuable asset, Akari. We cannot let you go. You are needed here…blah, blah, blah."

"Well, you surveilled me without my knowledge, so perhaps they're right."

"Hey, what can I say. I am Japanese, so I blend in. Have you tried the restaurant at the Marriott yet?"

"Room service for dinner when I checked in and then breakfast. Both were excellent, for hotel food."

Akari had a natural beauty about her. She appeared to be very health conscious and aware of her surroundings. Like many Japanese women with whom Delaney had interacted on prior investigations, Akari was another young woman in modern-day Japan, where life was extremely complicated. She had to navigate through a jumble of traditional values, modern society demands, and a plethora of choices. She was quick-witted and loved to have the last word. *Besides that,* Sean thought, *she's great looking, smells great, and is a perfect partner to be working with while tracking down the Black Cell.*

Chapter Eight

THE CALL FROM the FBI's equivalent of Internal Affairs came in a little before 9:00 a.m. the next day. "Agent Loomis?" A male agent asked.

"Yes, this is Agent Loomis."

"I'm Agent Terrance Reed with the Office of Professional Responsibility. I've been informed that your SAC, Lomax, alerted you to the nature of this phone call?"

"He did."

"Look, personally, I don't like this one bit, but it's my job."

"I understand, Agent Reed. So, what's the next step?"

"We'd like you to return to San Francisco so we can conduct an interview and collect your weapon and credentials. I assume you have them with you?"

"You're aware I'm on vacation."

Reed cleared his throat. "Yes, and if you refuse to return to the bureau until after your vacation, I can assure you it won't be held against you."

"I'm sorry, Agent Reed, but I find that to be a promise you personally can't keep with higher-ups able to overrule you. No, I was expecting your call and request. I'll be leaving Idaho in about fifteen minutes and can be in my office on Wednesday morning, say, 10:00 a.m?"

"Thanks for your cooperation, Agent Loomis. We'll see you there this Wednesday at ten. I'm sure you're aware of your rights to counsel at that time." Jeannie did not respond; she just hung up.

Fuck it, she thought. *I'm already accused of something I didn't do, so why not push the envelope. Let's see how fast I can make the trip home*. She looked at her watch. *A little over fifteen hours plus to get home if I follow the speed limits. But, with a few pee stops and food, and with the pedal to the metal, I bet I can make it in fourteen.*

She called the Idaho and Oregon State Police and the California Highway Patrol and notified them she would be exceeding the speed limit as a federal agent in urgent need of making it to San Francisco for a major investigation and driving a 2020 red Corvette.

How the hell does an FBI agent get the cash to buy a Corvette, they'll be asking themselves.

Throwing her suitcase and belongings into the car, she put a thermos filled with coffee on the passenger seat and hit the road, praying her route to the City-by-the-Bay would remain clear.

She called Lomax to let him know she got the IA call and was on her way back to California. Her plan was to make it home to Newark and get a good night's sleep before her interview at the bureau. Being pissed gave her energy.

During the first part of her trip, she tried to recall the particulars of the Dr. Hausser shooting. A descendant of the infamous doctor, Joseph Mengele of Auschwitz, Hausser was part of a secretive modern-day Nazi organization hoping to not only create a new Fourth Reich but clone infants with Adolf Hitler's DNA they had obtained from a Russian secret police (FSB) vault.

After an exhausting worldwide search for Hausser and his cronies, Jeannie's San Francisco team found documents referring to an unnamed island off the coast of Argentina where Hausser had lived in the past. A known associate, low-hanging fruit in the Nazi organization, was being held by the Hamburg police department. After his interrogation, which netted valuable information, Jeannie retreated to her room for the night.

At around 4:00 a.m., she woke and could not get back to sleep, so, dressing warmly, she took a walk around the surrounding Hamburg streets. During the walk, she was spotted, kidnapped, and flown to Hausser's island.

Homing in on Jeannie's cellphone, which had not been secured by her abductors, Delaney found the island's exact location, but by the time forces arrived and secured both the doctor's villa and hospital, Jeannie had been flown out. Playing on a hunch based on Hausser's attempt to replicate Hitler's life as an infant, Delaney found the doctor and Jeannie in Austria near Hitler's birth site.

When Delaney gained entrance to the residence where Jeannie was being held, Hausser emerged from a back bedroom carrying a Hitler clone. After placing the baby in a bassinet, he turned toward Delaney while holding a Walther P.38, and from there, everything went to hell.

Jeannie had been able to free herself from her bindings and rushed into the room where Hausser and Delaney were in a standoff. Hausser's nurse placed a cyanide capsule in her mouth and fell to the floor. Jeannie remembered bending over to check on her condition. That was when Hausser fired a shot, striking Jeannie in the shoulder. Delaney immediately returned fire, hitting Hausser in the upper arm. Turning toward Delaney, Hausser fired another shot at Jeannie, then turned back to Delaney, who was waiting. Sean fired two shots into Hausser's chest and another into his forehead. Jeannie had no weapon and, therefore, could not have fired a shot.

So why are they coming after me? She asked herself. During the mayhem, Hausser accidentally killed the infant with one of his wild shots. His nurse was dead from cyanide, and Delaney killed Hausser. The only other casualty was Jeannie. *So why me?*

Jeannie was making good time on her return trip to California. A few bathroom stops, refueling, fast food purchases, and listening to the end of her audiobook, *Hitting Rock Bottom*, made the time fly. It helped that the snow did not hit Idaho until after she passed into Oregon. A Corvette was not the type of vehicle one would want to drive in snow.

Her thoughts sometimes drifted to her recently discovered aunt and the inheritance she would be receiving. The whole affair was wrapped in mystery. An attorney in Fremont, California, notified her that her aunt, a person named Sylvia Nelson Kincaid, had died, and she was the sole beneficiary. She was slated to inherit over $3 million dollars, plus the aunt's cat.

She kept questioning herself during the drive. *How could Mom have a sister, my aunt, and never tell me about it? No one ever mentioned an Aunt Sylvia, nor were there any pictures of such a person when I went through Mom's boxes of old photos when I cleaned out her house. If Mom really did have a sister Sylvia, what could have happened to cause such a tragic falling out? And, how does this Paul Radcliff figure that attorney Goldstein mentioned fit into the puzzle? Is that why we never took a trip to the east coast while I was growing up?*

Finally, the sign indicating she had entered the Golden State came into view. Several more hours, and she would be home. After finishing the audiobook, she switched over to the news.

> ".....his wife found the congressman in his study when he did not come down for dinner. Congressman Emmet Carlson, a longtime politician, was pronounced dead at the scene. He was the victim of a self-inflicted gunshot. And now, a word from our sponsors...."

Huh! she thought. *That old fart's been in office for as long as I can remember. The last time I saw him, he was on television with a bunch of other damned progressives agreeing with the governor of this state that bathrooms should be gender-neutral. Good riddance, Emmet.*

Thank God I'm home. Now a hot shower and maybe a bowl of oatmeal, and off to dreamland. She set the alarm for 7:00 a.m., figuring that would give her enough time to have breakfast and get dressed before driving across the bridge. *If they want a fight, bring it on!*

Chapter Nine

TANAKA WAS ONCE again standing before his group of fellow hackers, presenting "A little update." He nodded toward Yuma, who unfolded a large piece of paper with **11 MILLION DOLLARS** written on it in large black print. "This is what we have removed from those we shall call The Corrupted. And this is from only two members of Congress in Phase Two. We have only just begun. I have decided to let the elites of the corporate world squirm for a little while longer and hold off our attack. Instead, let us have some fun," he said, laughing and rubbing his hands.

"Yuma will hand each of you a folder containing the name of a member of The Corrupted. I realize that this hack is child's stuff for all of you but remember our goal. Like modern-day Robin Hoods, we will lift the burden of the ill-gotten gains from their accounts and redistribute it to those in need. Of course, we must take care of ourselves as well." Everyone clapped, and some whistled.

Yuma made her way around the room. Everyone tensed as she approached, and the evil eye she gave them only intensified their discomfort. "Okay, let the fun begin. Drain their assets," Akio said as he left the room.

***

Akari asked if she could freshen up in Sean's room before going down for dinner. When she emerged from the bathroom, Sean was amazed at the transformation in her appearance. She had replaced her earlier garb with clothing from her backpack and was now wearing a silver-colored silk blouse and black slacks. The new outfit greatly enhanced her beautiful body. He felt a bit guilty lusting after her. *Another reason why I need to end it with Jeannie*, he thought.

"You clean up nicely. Must have been the whole motor scooter persona." Akari smiled.

"Are you ready for dinner?" she asked as she placed her backpack on his bed.

She sat across from Sean in the hotel dining room, sipping a glass of white wine while perusing the menu. "Gee, everything looks so good. Do you know what you are having?"

"I think I'll have the Kobe steak."

"That sounds good. I'll have it too." She folded her menu and handed it back to Sean.

The waiter noticed the exchange and quickly came to their table. "Can I take your order?"

As the waiter left, Akari reached into her purse and pulled out a sheet of paper. In the process, Sean could not help noticing her well-shaped breasts. *Delaney, you're sex-crazed,* he thought to himself.

"So, we have learned a little more about the Black Cell, but from what I hear, it was not easy to track down, nor is it complete. The term Black Cell has numerous meanings and references. There is even a company called Black Cell, a professional cybersecurity company that really snagged everyone's interest but turned out to be a dead end.

"Have you heard of the game *Game of Thrones*?" Not waiting for an answer, she continued. "In the game, Black Cells are a level of the dungeons of the Red Keep. They are reserved for prisoners accused of high crimes, like treason."

"I don't play video games. I find life much more appealing," Sean commented.

"As do I."

Is she flirting with me? Sean asked himself.

"In the *Call of Duty* video game, there is also a reference to Black Cell, but it's another dead end. In medical terminology, certain cancer cells are called Black Cells."

"This is all very interesting, but is it going anywhere?" Sean asked.

"Patience, big guy. Are you aware of the person who got all the credit for creating the Federal Bureau of Investigation, J. Edgar Hoover?"

"Quite before my time, but, yes, I'm aware of Hoover. How does he fit into our investigation?"

"Sean, some things are better when you go slow. Again, be patient."

That was a flirt without a doubt, he thought.

"In 2001, a hit movie called *Swordfish* starring John Travolta, Halle Berry, and Hugh Jackman hit the movie theaters. Did you see it? It was an action thriller, and I really liked it."

"Again, afraid not," Sean replied. "How does Swordfish relate to the term Black Cell?"

"Glad you asked. In the movie, a terrorist, played by Travolta, headed a secret organization that was supposedly created by the late J. Edgar Hoover, called the Black Cell. Its purpose was to launch retaliatory attacks against terrorists who threatened the United States. As I said, a good movie, but loose on facts.

"You see, Hoover actually did have a secret operation going on during his tenure. It was not called the Black Cell but went by the term Black Bag Operations or Black Bag Jobs. It was a very covert, clandestine operation where FBI agents, and lackeys they recruited, made illegal entries into denied areas. They used, by our standards today, old methods to gain entry like lock picking, safe cracking, key impressions, electronic surveillance, you know, audio and video bugs, and mail interception. Black Bag referred to the small bag burglars use to carry their tools. Now, whether the gang of hackers adopted this name from the movie is anyone's guess.

"Anyway, under Black Bag Operations, FBI agents entered the offices of targeted individuals and organizations and photographed information found in their records. This practice was used by the FBI from 1942 until 1967. In July 1966, FBI Director J. Edgar Hoover supposedly ordered the practice to be discontinued. The activities of Black Bag Jobs by the FBI were declared unconstitutional by the U.S. Supreme Court. The CIA has used Black Bag Operations to steal cryptography and other secrets from foreign government offices outside the United States and is still doing it."

"You said, 'supposedly.' I assume he continued the operation? Hoover, I mean?" Sean queried.

"Give the agent a gold star. Yes, he targeted anyone who disagreed with him, especially political enemies and individuals who thought they were above the law.

"Perhaps our Black Cell likes the best of Hoover's old program and the term used in the Swordfish movie. That is our best guess so far. Now for the really nitty-gritty stuff."

Before she continued, she waved at the waiter, asked for a list of dessert items, and ordered two more drinks from the bar.

Sean loved her commanding presence. She broke the mold of the more traditional

Japanese woman who generally refers decision-making to the male.

Referring to her paper, she also produced two photos. "We believe this is their leader. His name is Akio Tanaka," she said, handing him one of the photos.

Tanaka was young, sporting a bun hairdo, and apparently trying to grow a beard and mustache. His eyes appeared too close together, or he could have been squinting when the photo was taken. In some ways, he reminded Delaney of a young Bruce Lee. While he studied it, she pulled out a second photo. "This is his girlfriend, Yuma Masuta. Of the two, don't ever, and I stress ever, turn your back on her. She is deadly.

"I know you are aware that her father was high-up in the Yakuza organization. But were you told about the time he allowed his daughter to witness him skinning a man alive? Instead of being sick at the sight, she pouted at not being able to participate.

"Now, about Black Cell's motivation—we can only speculate. Money and power are probably part of it. Is that not what makes the world go round? And finally, their whereabouts. We have no clue. Our best idea is to locate Yuma and follow her to her residence or their hangout, but it won't be easy. I must tell you, solving this case would really help my career and make it possible for me to advance out of Japan."

After two more drinks, Sean was really feeling the effects. They took the elevator to his room so she could get her backpack. Before leaving, she leaned into Sean and gave him a light kiss on the lips. Her scent was particularly alluring. “Nice meeting you, Agent Delaney. I look forward to working with you. How about breakfast here at nine? She did not wait for a reply. Leaving, she glanced back at him while the door drifted shut.

Chapter Ten

CONGRESSWOMEN REBECCA BALDWIN was only forty-two years old, but she had been involved in politics since interning for Senator Bill Collins many years ago. A few blowjobs and intercourse on his desk helped her move up the ladder quickly, culminating in a seat in both Congress and on one of the most prestigious panels the Senate had to offer.

She refilled her glass with vodka and a little cranberry juice, then opened her laptop. A few keystrokes, and she was on the site where she could check her bank balance. She typed in her username followed by her password. Once the account filled the screen, she checked on the first of two accounts.

"That can't be right," she said out loud. She took another drink and started all over. Once again, the results were the same. *"What the fuck? Did I combine the two accounts together?"* Exiting the first account, she went to the second, which also showed a zero balance. She felt some sweat on her brow and searched for her phone. Once she found it, she had to return to her computer to find the bank's phone number.

After talking to two individuals, she finally reached the branch vice president, whom she asked to check her accounts since there was obviously a mistake. She had not withdrawn money in the last twenty-one days. Surely it had to be a banking error, or someone had hacked into her account. She demanded restitution but did not get it. The Black Cell had struck.

***

Jeannie woke just before the alarm went off and stretched. *Not too bad after such a long drive,* she thought. Wearing a San Francisco Giants long-sleeved t-shirt and boxer shorts, she visited the bathroom and relieved herself. Having slipped into her bathrobe and slippers, she walked downstairs, stopping at her aquarium to feed and say hi to her fish. "Did you guys and gals miss me?" There was no answer as they swarmed to the surface to grab food pellets she scattered across the top of the water.

Her cell rang, and she could see it was Ismail. "Hey, Ace. Catching any bad guys?"

"Hey, boss-lady. In fact, we just caught the old-man bank robber."

"No shit, really? Who was it? Did he have a jacket? How was he caught?

"Hey, slow down. I know on the outside I look like a prime male specimen, suave and extremely good-looking, not to mention brilliantly intelligent, but I'm getting old."

Jeannie laughed. She had missed the daily banter she and Ismail exchanged. "Actually, the dude is only forty-seven years old. He had a contact at an actor's makeup store, you know, wigs, makeup, shit like that, and that's how he made himself look older than he is. We didn't catch him. The credit goes to the Milpitas Police Department down by San Jose.

"Get this - The perp goes into a Bank of America and pulls the job. He leaves the bank and runs around the corner to the back parking lot while pulling off his mask. Two of Milpitas's finest, Barney Fife and his partner, are parked next to each other, shooting the shit. The idiot comes around the corner just as the dye packet goes off. Busted."

"How many jobs did he pull?"

"He admitted to seven, but he probably did more. He waited a day or so after pulling the robberies, then cruised up to the casinos in Lake Tahoe and Reno to clean the money in case any bills were marked. We got tapes from the casinos confirming his story."

"That's great. I wish we had more easy ones like that," Jeannie lamented.

"Hey, sorry to hear they're still putting you through the wringer. I'll bet it will be over today after the IA interview. It's all bureaucratic bullshit. You didn't even have a gun, so what's this shit all about?" Ismail asked.

"Wish I knew, buddy. I'm getting ready to head in for my interview and should be there in about an hour. Once I'm through, I'll track you down. Lomax suggested I not tell you too much because those assholes may drag you in as a witness. You know how that goes."

"Well fuck'em! I can take care of myself, but I understand Lomax's concern. Don't let the turkeys get to you. See you soon."

Jeannie glanced at her watch. Just enough time for another cup of coffee, and then she had to run. The doorbell rang. *God, it has to be Delores!* she thought. She opened the door, and sure enough, there stood Delores in a bright flowery bathrobe with oversized curlers in her hair. "Oh, hi Jeanie, you're back. How was your trip?" She strained to look around Jeannie for any signs of Delaney. Not seeing any, her focus came back to Jeannie.

"Yes, I came back last night, and I was just about to leave for an important meeting at the office, so I really have to run."

"Oh, okay then. I just wanted to make sure you know that Walter and I took good care of your fish and made sure your garbage was put out. Can you believe they're going to increase our bill again? What the hell is happening in this state? Gas, food, taxes. Is there no end? I told Walter, and I heard on the news last night that it's estimated that from July 2019 to July 2020, over 135,000 more people left the state than moved here. People are leaving because it's not affordable anymore, and don't get me started on that damn governor of ours."

Jeannie counted the minutes passing by in her head. *Damn, will my sweet, nosey neighbor ever shut up?*

"And twenty-three percent of California's voters reported they were seriously considering leaving California."

"Gee, I'm sorry to have to cut you off, Delores, but I really do have to make this meeting. Thank you so much, you and Walter, for taking care of everything while I was gone. When things get back to normal, I want to have you over for dinner."

"Oh, that would be so nice; just let us know when."

That said, Jeannie shut her front door, opened the garage, and quickly backed out, hoping not to run Delores over. She saw her in her rearview mirror, waving as she turned the corner.

Traffic on the approach to the Dumbarton Bridge was heavy. She soon passed a tow truck in the slow lane helping a stalled motorist. Fifty-five minutes later, she parked in the Bureau's secured parking lot and took the elevator to her floor, where she was greeted by her secretary. "How was your short vacation?" Jeannie blushed, thinking that maybe she was asking about her romantic getaway with Sean. Before she could answer, Ismail walked up with a cup of coffee.

"Is that for me?" Jeannie asked.

"Sure, why not," Ismail said, handing her the cup. "I already have to cover for you and do your job, so why not give you my coffee?" They laughed.

"No work to do?" SAC Lomax asked as he joined the group. "I'm on it, boss," Ismail said as he started his walk to Jeannie's office that was temporarily his.

"Got time to join me for a cup?" Lomax asked, turning and beginning to walk toward the breakroom, not waiting for an answer. Jeannie followed him. There was an agent sitting at the table, but when he saw the two enter, he said hi to both and made a quick exit. "I heard your interview's at ten this morning."

"Yes, and I think I'm ready. I hope that somehow I learn where this shit's coming from." On her drive to the city, she had felt anger for the first time, anger that she was suffering the consequences of Sean's actions, as righteous as they were.

"Look, like I told you," Lomax began, "The killing of Dr. Hausser brought repercussions to the Organization. Those Nazi assholes and their fucked-up hierarchy need to show they're still in charge, that they still have power. You're their scapegoat. Why they chose you and not Delaney is something I can't understand. I would've expected them to target both of you—but who knows, given their warped sense of the world. Just promise me you'll not go postal in there. Stay cool. They know it's a bunch of crap. Hell, you didn't even have a gun, so what are they investigating?

"There is no way our weak-ass president will capitulate to the Austrians' demand, although that may be debatable. It's all show. The problem is the president's numbers are falling like a lead balloon, and he needs to look strong. So again, just be cool."

"I promise. The agent who asked me to come in for the interview hinted they're just jumping through hoops and not to worry, but that could just be a good con job."

Chapter Eleven

"GOOD MORNING, AGENT Delaney. I hope you slept well?"

"Good morning to you, Akari. Fitfully, but eventually, yes." *Is she implying she should have stayed last night?"*

Delaney remained standing until Akari sat down. "Have you ordered already?" she asked.

"No, just coffee." The waitress approached their table and asked if Akari would also like a coffee, which she accepted. "So, have you solved the case, or do you need my expertise?"

"I need all the help I can get, especially after you saved me from getting killed in Yakuza territory yesterday," Sean replied. "This is your country, and as you said, I probably stick out like a sore thumb. I couldn't sleep after you left, so I made a few phone calls. Although the information you provided last night is very useful, we really needed more about the alleged leader of Black Cell, Akio Tanaka."

"And what, pray tell, did you learn?" she asked as she placed some cream in her coffee and stirred.

Delaney pulled a piece of folded stationery from his shirt pocket and began to read aloud. "Akio Tanaka is the only child of Yamato and Ishiro Tanaka. He was born in Nigata and excelled in school. Some of his instructors felt he was a savant, especially in mathematics. His grandfather was charged with war crimes after World War II, stemming from his 'Rape of Nanking' involvement. He received the death penalty and was supposed to be hanged by a military court. Someone smuggled in a knife for him, and he committed hara-kiri in his cell.

"Akio's mother couldn't handle the embarrassment and took her own life by hanging. Akio found her body when he came home from school. That appears to be his trigger since he began getting in trouble at school following her suicide. That's when his computer prowess began to show. His first venture was hacking into the school's grading system, awarding himself and his small circle of friends outstanding marks in all subjects. He was caught stealing memory chips from a store, and that was the last straw for his legal guardians."

Having come to the end of the bio, he commented to Akari, "He became, what we call in England, a ward of the state. He bounced around from one home to the other. If he weren't hacking into his guardian's bank accounts, he was siphoning money off various banking institutions. His criminal activity culminated in his incarceration when he reached adulthood, first at Fuchu and then Tochigi Prison. This is where the trail ends. No more information."

"Why? When he was released from Tochigi Prison, why isn't there any record of his release, you know, his residence, future place of employment?"

Sean smiled. "I'm afraid that can't be answered. You see, he wasn't legally released. Instead, he hacked into the prison computer system and gave himself an official early release date. The prison opened the gates, and he was on his jolly way, never to be seen again. It appears he just vanished." Silence hung over the table. "Huh. Resourceful guy. I wonder how his personality relates to Yuma?

"I never thought of that," Akari responded. "Maybe it is an idol worship thing. Or, maybe Akio is just good in bed."

I'll bet you're feisty in bed too, Agent Akari, Sean thought to himself.

"So, with all of this new information, what is your plan?" Akari asked, adding more sugar to her second cup of coffee. "I mean, no offense, but the information I gathered and what you just explained does not seem to get us any closer to the prize."

"No, but I still feel that Yuma Masuta is our only possible route to tracking Akio down."

"And how are we going to do that?" Akari asked.

"That's where you come in. I mean, you're a seven-year Interpol agent, correct?" Akari stuck her tongue out. "I know you have discrete contacts in her mother's neighborhood. We'll offer money for information about Yuma. Second, we'll arrange to have a bug placed in her mother's home as well as monitor her cellphone. All we need is a phone call from Yuma lasting long enough for us to trace her location, and we're one step closer."

***

Nancy Jefferson had been a member of Congress for over fifty-two years. It appeared that the older she got, the more liberal she became. Normally, it is the other way around; age often makes people more conservative in their worldview, but not her. Now in her early eighties, rumor suggested she was developing senile dementia. She had been photographed nodding off during congressional hearings, and when she was cornered by the media, her comments were laced with lapses of memory and misspoken information, much like our sitting president.

Adding her time in state government before entering Congress, she had been a public servant for sixty-two plus years. Given that and the income from her husband's Chinese dealings, the two had accumulated a massive amount of wealth, far exceeding what a Congresswoman would make. Of course, most of it was criminally earned and had to be sheltered in offshore accounts like their colleagues in both political parties, all of whom used the same offshore banking institutions.

Tired of press scrutiny, she and her husband decided to take an extended vacation to the Cayman Islands. Nothing like lying on the beach so close to one's money. On Tuesday morning, after arriving in Grand Cayman and in excellent moods, they hailed a cab and drove to the Cayman National Bank. Why not? How much interest had they accrued since they last checked? Not immediately noticed by anyone, the husband approached a young woman sitting at a desk positioned near the front door.

"Good morning. How can I help you?" she asked as they approached.

"My wife and I would like to check on our balance as well as our security box," John Jefferson replied.

"Very well. Please have a seat. I will need your identification, and after I locate your account, you will need to enter your password."

Mr. Jefferson had to pull out his passport as well as the password he carried in his wallet, not knowing it off hand. "Here you are," he said as he handed the passport to her. "Do you need my wife's also?"

Before answering, she had entered the information provided into the computer. "No, that won't be necessary. I see it is a joint account."

"Yes, it is," Nancy said, looking at her husband.

She turned the computer around to him and asked him to input the password. He did so and turned the computer back to her.

"Huh," the bank clerk said, with a puzzled look on her face. Without saying anything, she re-entered the information and had him re-enter the password, which brought up the same result. "Let's try this again with your wife's information if you don't mind." The results were identical.

"I'm sorry, Mr. and Mrs. Jefferson, this account has been liquidated and closed."

"Well, that's absurd! We never closed this account," he said, looking at his wife. "I need to speak with the bank manager, and I want to see him immediately."

***

"Good morning, Jeannie. I'm Steven Warner, your union attorney representative. I've asked the review board for a few minutes to discuss matters with you since you were on vacation, and we couldn't meet sooner. They've given us as much time as we feel is needed." Jeannie estimated that Warner, wearing a store-bought suit and Skechers dress shoes, was in his late twenties or early thirties. He combed his hair in a wavy pompadour style with tapered sides. *I'll bet he's a Justin Bieber fan,* Jeannie thought. *Looks like a real dick-wad.*

The two entered a small room off the main conference room. "I didn't contact the union or ask for an attorney," she told him.

"No, your SAC Lomax requested us. We told him the request had to come from you, but he was quite insistent and promised to raise a stink if we didn't comply. We told him we'd come today, but you can refuse our representation if you wish."

Lomax wants to make sure I don't put my foot in my mouth, go postal, and cut my own throat. "No, I'm glad you're here. I planned to represent myself, but a little voice in my head told me that it would be as foolish as a person trying to represent themselves in court. So, can you shed any further light on what this is all about?"

"Frankly, the higher-ups in our office are confused about the whole affair. Agent Lomax provided us with the Austria review team's findings of the shooting. It's documented that you didn't possess a weapon at the time of the shooting, so we can't understand the nature of this inquiry. Therefore, it's extremely important that you allow them to present their case before we offer anything in the form of a rebuttal. Agreed?"

Chapter Twelve

The Osaka Gas Company van arrived at around 8:20 in the morning. A worker got out and went to a corner house and knocked on the door. A brief conversation took place, and he was allowed entry into the home. About nine minutes later, he exited and went to the next house, that of Yuma Matsuta's mother.

"I am checking the homes in the area since we are getting reports of a possible gas leak. It will only take me a few seconds to make sure your home is OK." Akari was sitting on her motor scooter, keeping time to music on her iPhone while watching the activity. She saw the van arrive and the agent, wearing an Osaka Gas uniform, enter the first house. She tensed a little when she saw him enter Matsuta's mother's home but relaxed when he left, hopeful that the mission was successful. *In Yakuza territory, news travels fast, especially if an unknown intruder is about,* she thought.

She looked down at her opened backpack and turned on a small black device, instantly hearing someone walking in Matsuta's residence. Quickly starting her scooter, she left the area. A short distance away, she parked her bike and entered a corner apartment. She nodded at another male Interpol agent who was watching the house with binoculars and monitoring a tape recorder picking up the same sounds Akari had heard on her scooter. *Now, we wait.*

Sean answered his cell on the first ring. It was Akari. "Delaney, the bugs are in place, and we have a clear signal. Now, let us hope Yuma calls her mom. I will meet you back at the hotel in about an hour." Delaney agreed.

***

"Agent Loomis, Mr. Warner. Please, be seated." Jeannie did not recognize the voice as that of Agent Reed, the person she had talked to on the phone. "I'm Agent Kenneth Peterson, and this is Agent Harold Richardson. We're both from the Office of Professional Responsibility. If it's OK, we'd like to record this interview. You'll be provided with a copy if you wish." *What is this, a form of bait and switch? Agent Reed, so sincere on the phone about not wanting me to worry about a bullshit case, now throws an unknown agent at me!*

She was aware that even if she said no, and the tape recorder was put away, it was always possible to trick the accused by recording without their knowledge. *Tricks of the trade from Interrogation 101.*

"Let's begin," Agent Peterson said as he turned on the recorder. "For the record, my name is Agent Kenneth Peterson. With me is Agent Harold Richardson, Mr. Warner—sorry, I don't remember your first name?"

"Steven Warner, union attorney representative for Agent Jeannie Loomis."

"Thank you. Also present is Agent Jeannie Loomis, Assistant Special Agent in Charge of the San Francisco Bureau. First, Agent Loomis, thank you for your cooperation in cutting your vacation short and being here today." Jeannie neither replied nor smiled. Agent Peterson went over Jeannie's rights in concurrence with Warner before the interview started. Once the preliminaries were out of the way, the supposed case against Jeannie was laid out.

"Agent Loomis, it's alleged by the Austrian government that on the date in question, you, along with Interpol Agent Sean Delaney and another Interpol agent, raided a residence in their country and shot and killed a Dr. Hausser. In the ensuing gun battle, an infant was also killed."

Immediately raising an objection before Jeannie could react, Warner asked if this interview was being conducted as a criminal act; and in that event, he would advise Jeannie to terminate the interview until a criminal attorney could be contacted.

Peterson looked at his partner, who nodded. Jeannie interpreted this as an indication that Agent Richardson was the one in charge. "No, at this time, it's strictly related to the United States government's response to the Austrian government's request that Agent Loomis returns to Austria to answer their tribunal's questions."

"Point of reference—can that tribunal find people guilty or issue punishments for acts committed?" Warner asked.

"Were this to be an investigation into a criminal matter recommended by the Office of Professional Responsibility, Agent Loomis would have been properly notified and advised of her right to an attorney," Agent Richardson stated.

"Gentlemen, can I take a break and confer with Agent Loomis before we continue?"

It was agreed to take a 15-minute break since it was obvious that the interview's groundwork was still being established. Jeannie went into an adjacent room and looked at Warner.

"I smell a witch hunt," Jeannie said.

"As do I. We could be entering a minefield. I think we need to shake things up."

The two discussed their strategy and after reaching an agreement, re-entered the interview room.

"Thank you for allowing us a brief break. With what's been discussed so far, anything Agent Loomis states on record could be used against her in Austria. Austria could perhaps recommend criminal prosecution for this absurd allegation that she shot and killed the victims when, and I'm sure you're both aware, she wasn't armed and, in fact, was wounded herself."

"That would be outside the scope of our investigation. But, yes, that's a possibility," Agent Peterson said.

"Therefore, I believe that in Agent Loomis' best interest, we'll request that this interview be terminated, and if she receives any form of consequences for that decision, we'll have her criminal representative take up the matter."

Jeannie remained silent during this whole discourse. She was getting sick to her stomach as the whole affair seemed to have morphed into a possible criminal indictment. *Holy shit, I could not only lose my job but also face incarceration.* She was impressed with Warner's ability to quickly realize the possible consequences of anything said during the interview.

Richardson reached over the table and shut off the recorder. "Agent Loomis and Mr. Warner. I'd like to talk to you off the record and assure you that all recordings have been turned off in this room. What I'm about to share, I would never admit to. If you would like, Agent Loomis, you can check and confirm this."

Jeannie still did not say a word. "That's the purpose for going off the record, assuming that's what we're doing?" Warner asked. All heads nodded in agreement.

Richardson folded his arms and leaned forward on the table. "Look, everyone in this room knows this is a bunch of bullshit. We, (pointing to Peterson), have read the shooting team's report. It was a clean shoot, and Agent Loomis had absolutely no involvement in the killing of either Hausser or the infant. Neither of us wants to be here. We currently have a weak president in office who's drowning in his low poll numbers. His party is second-guessing their choice of having him elected, if he truly was, and representing their party. The vice-president might be even worse if the president resigns for health reasons."

"There's no love lost between him and the president of Austria. The hatred between the two goes way back to when the president was a senator. He got caught on a hot mic referring to her as a sour puss Nazi. She's never forgiven him. The Austrian government knows he's weak. They're hoping he'll give in to their request for extradition."

"So, you both feel this is coming from the president of Austria as retaliation for a comment made years ago?" Warner asked. It was a question Jeannie wanted to ask.

"No, she's just a pawn in this whole affair. Agent Loomis and Agent Delaney stirred up a hornet's nest in Europe and around the world during their investigation of Dr. Hausser and his cloning experiments for the Nazis. Our intelligence agencies are aware of the "Fourth Reich's" existence, their "Organization," as they call it, and their ambition to rise again and secure world dominance. The Austrian president just wants to survive her term in office and, like a puppet, will comply with any demands the Organization places on her."

"Why they decided to focus on Agent Loomis and not the other two Interpol agents present that day, we don't know. Maybe the Organization has other plans for them, but they're not our concern." Stillness filled the air for several moments.

Jeannie felt that both agents were being sincere and put to rest her thoughts of being baited with the replacement of Agent Reed with Peterson. *Are they coming after me because I'm a woman, or is it, as they stated, the Organization taking offense due to our weak, senile president? Neither of these two agents can promise anything. The final action will happen in D.C.*

Warner leaned forward, resting his elbows on the table. "Here's what I'm proposing. We'll stipulate that Agent Loomis's statements go on the record, taped. And if it's not agreed that it'll be handled in this manner, the interview will stop, and a criminal attorney will take over.

"All that will be required from Agent Loomis is for her to walk us through the events of that day, step-by-step, just like she did for the shooting team. She's already been cleared by the FBI, and her words on tape will just re-emphasize her lack of culpability. Anytime she feels uncomfortable regarding any questions the two of you may ask, she or I will raise our hand, and the recorder will be shut off. If you'd both like to discuss this privately, the two of us can use the time for a bathroom break."

Chapter Thirteen

TWO DAYS HAD passed, and Delaney was starting to get bored and frustrated. Yet, there appeared to be no other avenues down which to pursue the whereabouts of Yuma and Akio. No phone calls were made or received by Yuma's mother. She appeared to have few friends. General banter was picked up between her and her neighbors on occasion, but Yuma was never mentioned.

Solving this case would go far in supporting Delaney's request to leave the desk-bound job he had in San Francisco and get back into the field. He had got past the death of his wife and felt ready to go back into the trenches. In some ways, he felt that both the director and deputy director had insinuated as much. *Look at this case,* he thought to himself. *International criminals striking fear into society. As Ismail would probably throw out there that this is James Bond stuff.*

Akari also grew bored and decided that staying around the same location on her scooter or apartment would, or already had, attract Yakuza attention. She decided to pull back and leave her team in place to do the monitoring.

Delaney called her around noon and asked if she would like to meet for lunch at a streetside café near his hotel. He didn't particularly want to discuss the case. Instead, he wanted to spend time with her. "You know, Agent Delaney, this might be taken as a form of sexual harassment," Akari said, kidding.

And what might the consequences of that be?" he replied, suppressing a laugh, thinking she was really hot for his body.

"It depends on how well you can carry out your sexual innuendos. See you at noon."

Delaney decided a visit to the bar might be what he needed. Exiting the elevator, he was headed toward the dining area when a porter approached him and said there was a package for him at the desk. Sean handed him a generous tip and followed him to the reception desk.

"You have a package for me? Sean Delaney, room 304."

"Yes, sir, here you go." The female receptionist handed him a manila envelope that, from the feel, appeared to contain papers. It had not only been sealed but taped securely. He found a booth and sat down, not feeling guilty for occupying it instead of a barstool since the bar was empty except for a businessman nursing what appeared to be a Manhattan. He ordered his usual, a vodka martini on the rocks with three olives. *Ismail probably would have said I should say, "Shaken, not stirred,"* he quietly said to himself with a smile.

He waited until his cocktail was served before opening the package. Inside was a picture of an overweight, young Japanese female with long black hair. The back of the photo had the name Yuma Masuta. It was a different picture than the one he'd seen before. Even though her hair was black, it appeared to have an almost purplish hue in the photo. Three pages were stapled to the photograph. He removed the staple, placed the photo back in the envelope, and began to read.

- Yuma Masuta. Twenty-one years old, 5'5", 155 lbs.
- Last known address was her parents' home in Osaka, Japan.
- Masuta's father was a member of Yakuza.
- Involved in extortion, smuggling, blackmail, running of prostitution rings, drug trafficking, restaurants and bars, and many other businesses in Japan.
- Father died seven years ago.

Nice background information, but I saw the same shit during my HQ briefing. He continued to read.

- Yuma formed the equivalent of an all-female Yakuza.
- Recent information gleaned from various intelligence sources claims she is responsible for eleven homicides.
- Preferred method of killing: stabbing following extensive torture.

Delaney pulled the photo out again and studied it with the new information in mind. *You really are a stone-cold killer, aren't you?* He ordered a second drink and after taking a few sips, realized that noontime was approaching. Placing the documents and photo back in the envelope, he folded it and put it in his jacket pocket to share with Akari over lunch and cocktails.

***

"To date, we have amassed over thirty-five million dollars from the Corrupted during Phase Two." Everyone in the room began to clap or whistle. Akio raised his hand, "But, we have not put a dent in the Corrupted's financial coffers. Each of you has a file that I would like you to study. Unfortunately, this is all we currently have on either the Republican or Democratic National Committee's financial accounts.

We do know that between these two parties, there are well over one-hundred billion dollars."

More hoots and small talk emanated from the hacker group. Yuma circled through them, making sure everyone had a file and that they were concentrating on what Akio was saying. "I want each of you Black Hats to attempt entry into their systems. Their files are all heavily encrypted and have excellent security systems, but I know your talents. Find that backdoor to their ill-gotten fortunes so we can eventually rid them of this burden." He laughed out loud and was joined by the group. Only Yuma did not exhibit emotion. She looked at the females in the group. "OK, get started, and a prize awaits the first person who breaks in."

***

Akari arrived at ten minutes past noon. She was no longer wearing her normal street clothes and had changed into something more revealing. Delaney stood as she approached. "You look stunning if that statement is allowed in your country without being labeled sexist."

"It is my opinion, Agent Delaney, that females who object to such a compliment are generally too ugly to receive one, and that is why they lash out." She smiled at her statement and turned her attention to the menu already in front of her.

"That's refreshing to hear," Sean said as he reached into his pocket, pulled out the envelope, and handed it across the table to Akari. "The latest intel. I'm afraid it's not much."

The waitress shortly arrived and took their order. Delaney selected a fish dish while Akari chose mushroom chicken. Looking at the documents, Akari agreed that most of it was just useless repetitive background information. "So, tell me, why did you join Interpol?" Delaney asked.

"The CIA would not take me. Just kidding." She swallowed some food and looked at Sean for a few moments. "Do you really want to know my background, Agent Delaney?"

"Only on two conditions. One, you stop calling me Agent Delaney and call me Sean, and second, only if you want to share."

Pausing as she played with the maraschino cherry in her old fashioned cocktail, she responded. "You already know how old I am, and I am sure you have determined my height and weight." With a flirtatious smile, she continued. "I graduated from the University of Tokyo at the top of my class. I majored in Law and Politics, hoping it would earn me a well-paid and secure job in government." Smiling, she began again after a brief pause, "Sean, it may seem to those outside Japan that we are a modern cultural society where women are entitled to the same status as their male counterparts. That is not reality. It is still a very misogynistic country. I learned at an early age what it was like to be groped while riding our subway systems. If you report such an incident, nothing will happen to the guilty. We women must just accept it.

"My female professors tried to persuade us women to push back and be more outspoken against the prevailing misogynistic practices, but doing so quickly gets you labeled, and your career choices become very limited. I see you are neither sleeping nor snoring, so I will continue."

"Please do."

"You know, Sean, you are a very attractive man. Not only in your looks but in the way you carry yourself. This is not customary in Japanese men."

"I will take that as a compliment." *She's definitely laying it on,* he thought.

"So, since I would not sleep with the CEOs of companies where I sought employment, I chose Interpol with the hopes of world travel, excitement, and the possibility of advancement. So, here I am. A dedicated agent of Interpol, yet still trapped at the Japanese field office."

"Never married? No children?"

"No, I have not sought a marriage partner so I could start a family. I did not want that to hinder the possibility of advancement or transfer to another country. How about you, Sean?"

Before answering, he smiled and ordered them both another drink.

Chapter Fourteen

AFTER A BRIEF break, everyone agreed to proceed with the interview. Agent Peterson made sure their comments were being recorded, and the interview commenced. As promised, no questions strayed from the actual day-of-interest events. Everything was straightforward, and Jeannie answered the same way she had during the shooting team's questioning. About an hour and ten minutes later, the interview was concluded.

"Thank you for your cooperation, Agent Loomis," Richardson said. "I don't think you'll hear from either of us again, but I can't promise what the State Department will do next. What I can say is that our report will conclude that there's no basis for this to proceed. But again, it's out of our hands. Unfortunately, however, you'll continue to be suspended with pay until the matter's finally resolved.

"I hope Mr. Warner will file a complaint about the suspension, but I don't think it'll be successful. My recommendation is for you to take a long and well-deserved vacation, and this will undoubtedly be what your SAC will order. Good luck, and we're sorry you're having to go through this."

Well, it seems that this interview was just a smoke screen. These two agents never did have the power to make this all go away. Now, I'll have to wait for God knows how long for those pieces of shit-swamp dwellers to decide what to do next, without any regard for my well-being. Well, bring it on, fuckers!

Jeannie shook hands with both agents and Warner. Richardson said he would be in touch if he heard anything. She walked out of the interview room and down the hallway toward her secretary, trying to ignore the stares from those who knew something was up. She finally arrived at Lomax's office. He looked up from his desk and motioned for her to come in and close the door. "Everyone must think I'm in deep shit, and I am," she said to Lomax.

"Well, how did it go?"

"Actually, not bad. They both leveled with me and my union rep. By the way, thank you for arranging that." Lomax did not reply. "You were right. According to Internal Affairs, this shit is coming from the Organization, those fucking modern-day Nazis.

The president of Austria is not much stronger than you-know-who in the White House. She just wants to ride out her tenure in office and then go off into the land of Schnapps and Schnitzel, or whatever the hell they drink over there. They're also at a loss as to why Sean wasn't targeted."

"I'm doing my damnedest to find that out. I'm calling for a lot of owed favors, but so far, zilch. Did they tell you the bad news?" Lomax asked.

"Bad news? About how long this bullshit's going to take, or the fact that I'm restricted to staying in this damned state? Is that what you're about to tell me?"

"Yes. Look, you and your team have busted your asses and solved some heavy-duty crimes. I wish I could give all of those involved an extended paid vacation, but Washington would have my ass. Bummer that you've got to stay in California. But hell, start in the northern part of the state and work your way south. There's a lot to see. You always said you wanted to see the country. Start with California. And you've long wanted to put a koi pond in your backyard. Now might be the time."

***

Delaney wasn't sure if it was the hum of the bar's air conditioner or just boredom, but he lost count of the number of drinks he and Akari downed. It was almost 2:30 in the afternoon when they left the café. They did not speak to each other as they navigated themselves back to Sean's hotel room. Once in the room, Sean stretched, trying unsuccessfully to rid himself of a low back spasm. Akari offered to give him a shiatsu, a Japanese massage that is a form of acupressure that follows the meridian lines of the body to transfer energy. Sean accepted. He removed his shirt and pants and then laid face down on the bed.

Out of the corner of his eye, he noticed and heard Akari taking off her blouse and skirt. Placing the articles on a chair, she climbed onto the bed and straddled Delaney. He felt the warmth of her thighs against his legs and thought he could feel her honey spot move back and forth on his rear as her strong hands massaged his area of pain.

Feeling relieved, he turned over to face Akari, who continued to straddle him. She was wearing a blue-colored bra and matching panties. She looked at Sean and then reached around and unsnapped her bra. She lowered herself and kissed Sean on his chest, eventually working up to his waiting lips. As the kissing intensified, they both found themselves nude, ready for the act of intimacy. Every possible position was explored, with both bringing so much energy into the act that they climaxed together, ending with Akari, now in the missionary position, falling asleep.

Sean realized he felt no shame for his lovemaking with Akari or for what he had shared with Jeannie. Maybe his transgression was due to being so many miles away from Jeannie with a new and exotic woman. Perhaps it was because he knew, deep inside, that he could not have a long-term relationship with Jeannie when he returned; he could not be a one-woman man. He recalled several of the affairs he had had while his wife lay dying. Even then, he justified his actions as a man needing intimacy. He just wrote it off as lust.

***

Jeannie tracked Ismail down, and the three walked to their favorite IHOP restaurant. "So, before you ask, as I told the boss—yes, the hearing went well."

"Well? How could those damned leeches even act like this was a legitimate hearing? You had no gun. You were cleared by our shooting team. It's all bullshit. You should've told them to go fuck themselves. Sorry boss."

"Relax, buddy. I think I have this under control. The boss here has been a great asset to me. It's all politics, and you know how much I hate politics. But, you know, after years of flying under the radar, politics always seems to find a way to bite you in the ass."

"Well, you do have a nice ass. Oops, sorry again, boss." Lomax just shook his head.

"Sexual harassment will get you everywhere," Jeannie said, laughing. "But thanks for the compliment. Anyway, they told me this case could drag on forever, so I'm taking the boss's suggestion, no, his order, to take an extended vacation, especially since it's with pay."

"Hey, how do I get something like that?" Ismail jokingly asked.

"You'll get your chance. IA will eventually catch up with you," Jeannie said, joining Lomax in laughter. Ismail and Lomax ordered a short stack of pancakes; Jeannie ordered a hot turkey sandwich.

"So, any ideas on what you'll do with your time off?" Lomax casually asked.

"Yeah. I think I'm going to see the state. I'm going to start up in Eureka and work my way down toward Mexico. I'm thinking of taking the coastal route. And, if I'm still suspended when I return, I'll get bids on putting in a backyard koi pond."

"Well, good for you. I think Agent Flores here can handle the job while you're gone, right Ismail?"

"Absolutely, sir."

Lomax finished his third cup of coffee and left them at the restaurant.

"You want to know how you get a sweet deal like a long-paid suspension? Shoot someone without having a gun and piss off modern-day Nazis, that's how," Jeannie said.

"Well, what are you going to do after your California trip? Watch sweaty contractors dig a hole in your backyard? Hey, maybe you can take up knitting or crochet? Hey, I know, you can take up golf. Maybe play down at Mar-a-Lago with former President Trump. He might remember you from the award he gave us after we killed those terrorists trying to blow up the BART tube."

"Boy, you're on a roll. Must have gotten lucky last night! Your poor wife, having to put up with you."

"What do you mean. She loves all of this," Ismail said, pointing to his body. "This is all USDA prime, right here."

Chapter Fifteen

Jeannie started her Corvette and left the bureau's secured parking garage. She took her time driving down Highway 101 toward the Dumbarton Bridge, contemplating what the hell she was going to do with all her free time. If Sean were available, they could drive to Monterey and then down to San Diego as Lomax had suggested. She had never been to Catalina Island. *That could be fun*, she thought. For the time being, that was out of the question since Sean was knee-deep in the Black Cell hacking investigation. She had still not told anyone about her inheritance and her newly found aunt, not to mention the cat. She was so deep in thought that she failed to notice a black SUV following her.

You know what, fuck the bureau. I'm on paid leave, and I haven't been charged with a crime, so why am I confined to this socialist state? What kind of justice is that? That's it! Time for a road trip to Myrtle Beach, South Carolina. I can continue to help the Idaho State Police. That killer of theirs needs to be caught.

***

Sean woke the next morning alone in bed. Reaching for his Omega watch, he saw that it was almost 8:30 a.m., late for him. He lay there for a few moments and smelled her scent on his pillow. *What did she say it was called? Peaches and Cream. That's it!*

Finally, he rolled out of bed and got in the shower, where he noticed that his BLV Notte shower gel had been moved. *Huh!* Nearing the end of an extended hot shower, he realized his back pain was gone. He called Akari's room, but there was no answer. Famished, he headed to the hotel dining room and found her sitting in a corner booth. She waved as he approached.

"Good morning, Agent Delaney," she said with a smile. "I mean, Sean."

"Good morning to you, sunshine. You got up early. I was disappointed to find you weren't next to me."

"Nothing gets past you field agents. By the way, I have something for you." She pulled out a gift bag from behind her and handed it to him. Somewhat heavy, Sean knew it was not more paperwork about Yuma from the agency.

"And what's this?" he asked.

"You mean field agents can't see through things?" she laughed.

He opened the bag and found a wrapped box containing a new bottle of his shower gel. "Now I know why the gel was moved in my shower."

"Hey, what can I say. I loved the fragrance while we were making out and decided you need to keep wearing it—at least, while you are in Japan with me."

"I think we did more than just make out, but I'm not complaining. Not one bit."

"Regrets, Agent Delaney?"

"None whatsoever. Perhaps we can continue to investigate the possibilities."

"Perhaps. I think we have an unspoken understanding of each other. By the way, do you always sleep with a gun under your pillow?"

Sean just nodded his head, thinking, *How can I respond? Yes, in my job with Special Branch, I have had to kill people, and now I am paranoid and keep a weapon under my pillow. Too much information.*

They ordered breakfast and were nearly through when Sean's cellphone rang. Akari could tell from the nature of the conversation that they may have gotten their first break in the case. Shutting off the phone, he said, "She finally called her mom. We can listen to the conversation when we get to the apartment, and the techs think she was on the phone long enough for us to determine her location. Let's go."

***

"Alright, everyone. Shut the fuck up," Akio shouted, obviously a little agitated. Yuma also seemed more demanding when talking to the group. "Today, we will drain the assets of the Republican and Democratic National Committees. Thanks to our red-headed Natasha, who found a way into their banking records, we will strike a blow to the Corrupted. Those arrogant bastards have so many accounts spread out worldwide that I will need everyone's best expertise to transfer their wealth to those more needy, but I digress. The redistribution of their wealth will start once they are left with nothing. It is time to begin the festivities. We are still in Phase Two. Now, let the mayhem begin."

***

NSA director Paul Falconer was feeling the pressure. He had just returned from a heated meeting at the White House where his ass was chewed and re-chewed. He did not have to deal with the president, whom he would have preferred to meet. He was so senile he could hardly put two sentences together. Literally shitting his pants was becoming a daily part of his life. *Hell, I bet Walmart has offered to direct ship Depends to the White House.* It was sad to see him having to play the role of president when instead he should have been enjoying his remaining years.

No, Falconer was not that lucky. Instead, he had to deal with the bitch from hell, Margaret Jennings, head of the State Department. Spawned from Satan himself, this career politician was another creature from the swamp called Washington D.C.

"Mr. Falconer. Thanks for coming here on such short notice. Please have a seat." Next to her was her ass-kissing lackey, Peter Townsend. Rumor had it he was bi-sexual, taking care of Margaret and anyone else who needed his services. When they were investigating Epstein and his sex island, Townsend's name was among those who visited frequently. "We have a delicate matter to discuss with you today. We believe it's related to the Super Bowl hacking investigation you're handling, although it appears you have nothing to show for your efforts." She let that statement hang in the air. Falconer decided not to respond since no matter what he said, he could not deny they had made no progress in the case. "What I'm about to tell you must remain in this room. Is that understood?"

"Crystal clear," Falconer responded, but thinking, *I can guarantee that leaks to the mainstream media will start when I leave!*

"Good," Jennings said and continued. "Early this morning, and then later this afternoon, both the Republican and Democratic National Committees' bank accounts were drained of all assets. Billions with a capital B are missing, and your agency must find it immediately. Do I make myself clear?"

***

Taking separate vehicles, Sean and Akari arrived at the apartment with the monitoring station. "The call came in about forty-five minutes ago," the agent reported and then pushed the recorder's play button.

"Hello, mother. How are you"?

"I am fine, daughter, and you?"

"Fine. Do you need anything? I can arrange for a delivery."

"No, I do not need anything. Mrs. Osaki brings me groceries when I need anything. I am sorry you could not come here to celebrate your birthday. When will you come and visit me?"

Sean and Akari listened intently, hoping that Yuma would commit to a visit in the future. They were disappointed.

"I am sorry, Mom, but right now, I am very busy in my career. Father would have been proud of me. I am making very good money and soon will help you move to a beautiful place where we can live together."

"But there is nothing wrong with this place, daughter. I am old and do not think I could handle a move."

"Mother, you would not have to do anything. I will arrange for everything to be moved for you. You and I can go on a long visit to the country. Would you like that?"

The conversation continued for a few more minutes. Yuma did not seem to care that she was on the line long enough to be traced. It appeared to

Delaney that she did not feel her phone calls were being monitored. He could not tell if Yuma felt she was under surveillance.

Before Sean and Akari arrived, one other member of the monitoring team ran a trace and found the phone was indeed a "throw away."

"The call pinged off this tower. That is the best we are going to get,"

Akari said as she looked at the area circled in red. "That is deep inside Yakusa-controlled territory. It will not be easy to flush her out, but I do have a few contacts and confidential informants in that area, so we can put out our feelers. I am afraid you will still stick out in that area. Japanese agents must do the work." She winked at Sean.

Finished with the map, Akari said, "Let's meet back at the hotel this evening. I will make a few contacts in that area, and later, we can come up with a plan."

Sean walked her outside and then grabbed her, spinning her around and bringing her close to him. He kissed her and said, "Yes. We're going to finish this together. Please be careful." Akari turned and walked to her scooter. *This job is murderous on relationships,* he thought as he made his way to his car.

Chapter Sixteen

"Hi, Delores. I have a big favor to ask you and Walter. I'm afraid I'll be gone again for a little while." Delores eagerly volunteered to watch over Jeannie's house, take care of her fish and the garbage, and make sure no burglars got in. Jeannie and her now-deceased fiancée used to joke about her nosy neighbor, but God love her; if someone wanted their house to be secure during an absence, Delores was the go-to person.

With all her bills handled online, Jeannie believed she should be fine away from home for up to a month, or maybe even two. She packed as much clothing as her sportscar would hold, which wasn't much, and left at 5:00 a.m. As much as she hated social media, the question she had posted about the best way to get to Myrtle Beach helped her decide to take the southern route. She would first head toward

Southern California, then go through Arizona, New Mexico, Texas, Oklahoma, Alabama, Georgia, and finally, South Carolina: a total of 2,817 miles. Google indicated it would take 42 hours. *How the hell do they estimate that?* she wondered. *A person needs to pee, don't they?*

Jeannie wasn't sure what she hoped to find in Myrtle Beach; maybe just answers to questions like why her mom and dad never mentioned an aunt.

***

"Today, we will partially reveal ourselves to the world," Akio began. "The media has kept it secret that the Republican and Democratic party's coffers have been emptied. Thanks to Margo (pointing to a female with spikey yellow hair and so many piercings she would fail an airport metal detector), we now have access to all mainstream media outlets and the larger cable channels. In a few moments, we will cut into the president's State of the Union address and prevent them from blacking us out. Today, my brother and sister hackers, the Black Cell becomes famous and feared at the same time."

At one minute past six-o'clock PST, everyone in the room focused on Akio, who was standing in front of a monstrous big-screen monitor. He looked at Yuma and nodded. There was a moment of snow on the screen, and then Akio appeared wearing a Vendetta mask. He began to speak:

> "Ladies and gentlemen of the world. This is the Black Cell. For too long, the media has controlled all your thoughts and actions. Dr. Joseph Goebbels knew this, and so did Adolf Hitler and every dictator that has come down the pike. They knew that a lie repeated often enough would eventually be believed by the masses as the truth. Why do you think you are constantly bombarded with commercials telling you what toothpaste will give you the brightest smile, what beer is the best, and, more significantly, who you should vote for? You are told what car you should drive. You are brainwashed into buying your favorite team's sportswear, only to have your team change colors or their name down the line, forcing you to buy a whole new wardrobe. Remember how they told us the world was ending due to global warming? And, on those rare occasions when the media is caught in a lie, they quickly change their narrative.

These elite individuals are found in politics, entertainment, sports, and business, and they all collude on what message, what narrative should be disseminated to you, the common person, the little person. God forbid you debate their righteousness. You will be labeled as a racist, fascist, or whatever term they all agree to use.

For the past several months, my family of Black Hats have started to rectify this situation. First, we showed you our power when we interrupted your championship football game, but that was just to demonstrate Black Cell's reach. Since that event, numerous politicians, sports figures, actors, and the elite we refer to as the Corrupted, have had their bank accounts liquidated.

You have not heard about this because they could not go to law enforcement and report the thefts. "Why?" you ask. Because they would have to explain how they accumulated so much wealth. And how did they? Through illegal means. Drug smuggling and sales. Sex trafficking, especially children. Stock market manipulation. Weapon sales. Think of a crime the average citizen would go to prison for and multiply the seriousness of that activity ten-fold.

And, if they are caught, which is a rarity, all the other Corrupted go into overdrive to protect them, spinning the narrative away from the guilty.

I'm sorry, ladies and gentlemen of this planet. I get carried away sometimes. Yesterday, we drove a stake through the heart of both leading American political parties by invading both their monetary holdings. The billions we removed will soon be distributed to those most in need. I guess you could say we are like the fictional character Robin Hood and his merry men and women.

Why are we doing this, you will ask? The answer is simple—power. I now have the power to control the far corners of the globe, not for higher profits, but for a higher understanding among the people of this planet.

And what do I expect in return? Worldwide domination. Complete, utter, total global domination. But not over a religion or ideology, over tyranny and isolation and true news and communication.

Today, I reveal my declaration of principles, a promise to the men and women of this planet, my brothers and sisters whom I humbly serve. Our social media will report world news without fear or favor. I promise Black Cell will be a force for good in this world, fighting injustice, crushing intolerance, battling inhumanity, and striking a blow for freedom and economic equality.

Caesar had his legions, Napoleon had his armies, and I have my hackers, my Black Hats. By midnight tonight, I will have reached and influenced more people than anyone in the history of this planet except for God Himself. All Jesus did was sermonize from a mount. Before I leave you, here are the names of the Corrupted who have already had their secret funds liquidated by Black Cell. Ask yourself this question, "How did they accumulate so much wealth?"

A rolling list of names, some with pictures, appeared on the screen alongside the dollar amount seized. Congressmen and congresswomen, sports figures, actors, actresses, and many of society's elite. At its conclusion, Akio re-appeared.

"*Good night, and peace out.*"

Chapter Seventeen

DELANEY RETURNED TO the hotel with the map, although he wondered while walking to his car what good it would do. He was way out of his element. Back at the hotel, he checked for messages but had none. A televised soccer match was in progress in the bar, so he stopped, ordered a drink, and thought about how helpless he felt. *I stick out like a sore thumb. This should have been assigned to one of our Asian agents, not some Brit. As soon as I walk out of the hotel, people notice me. Yuma, our only lead, is holding up the whole investigation. Catch that bitch, and we may get our first break.*

Glancing at his watch, he wondered why he had not received any updates from Akari. Needing something to eat since breakfast had not satisfied him, he ordered a burger and fries to eat at the bar. He learned that a second game would be on soon featuring Manchester United, so hanging out in the bar waiting for her call was better than sitting in his room.

Just before the Manchester United game started, the screen was taken over by someone in a mask. He knew it had to be Akio. The bartender started to change channels, but Delaney asked him to stop and even asked for an increase in volume. He listened intently to Akio's words, hoping to better understand the Black Cell operation's motivations. *A typical egomaniac who believes the whole world revolves around him and that he's the center of the universe. Sure, he promises the redistribution of wealth, but I bet a considerable amount ends up in his pocket. It always does with these assholes.*

At the conclusion of the televised message, Sean's cellphone rang. He answered, hoping it was Akari. Instead, it was Interpol headquarters in Tokyo. They, too, had witnessed Akio on the air and asked Sean to come in for a briefing in three hours. He glanced at his watch and decided to call Akari for an update. The phone rang, but there was no answer. *She must still be out and about.*

Then a thought hit him like a thunderbolt. *What if Akari is a double agent? What if she's a Yakuza mole placed inside Interpol. No wonder they've been unsuccessful in tracking Yuma or finding the Black Cell's location. She was feeding them all our intelligence. That's why they seem so elusive. Damn, why didn't I see this sooner?*

***

"Where is Yuma?" Akio asked when he entered the room. "We have much to do today."

No one offered the whereabouts of his partner. "Margaret, call her and find out where the hell she is." He returned to his office and looked at a list of non-profit organizations about to receive a sizeable donation to increase their bottom line.

The list of non-profits included churches, public schools, public charities, public clinics and hospitals, legal aid societies, volunteer service organizations, labor unions, professional associations, research institutes, museums, and a few carefully selected governmental agencies. Care had to be taken to assure that funds could be deposited but never traced back to the sender. It was child's play for his Black Hats; it really didn't matter to Akio. Phase Four was his primary objective: *Siphoning funds from the world's largest bank. Wow!*

Beside that list was a computer printout of coding related to all branches of the U.S. military and the Pentagon. *This will be Phase Three. Bring the world to the brink of a nuclear war. It will distract from our bank assault.*

***

"It makes no sense to scream, you fuckin' bitch. You are in a soundproof room. No one will hear your screams, and soon, you will not be able to do so anyway. I will make you very comfortable," said Yuma picking up a syringe. Three other females were in the room. Akari had been stripped naked and was lying on her back atop a steel table.

Walking toward Akari with the syringe, Yuma tapped the solution inside. "Do you know what curare is? No? Let me tell you. It is a paralyzing poison used by many indigenous South American people and a very powerful muscle relaxant. Its paralytic effects used to be used for surgical procedures in which complete cessation of movement was necessary. It has been replaced by other agents now, but I have found it very useful in torture. My curare is a blend of different herbs, still immobilizing the subject but allowing them to speak and scream." Yuma could see the terror in Akari's eyes.

"I can't take the credit for knowing about this curare derivative. It was something my father introduced me to. Seeing his victims totally paralyzed, yet awake, watching their body parts be removed until sadly they died. It was so exhilarating." She injected the solution into Akari's neck. "It will take effect very quickly."

Yuma talked with her female compatriots, joking and laughing until her attention again returned to Akari. "How do you feel? Can't move? That's OK. You can still feel and watch, but I'm afraid you will no longer be able to scream.

"Have you heard of the ancient art of Chakra Torture? According to Eastern philosophy, the body has seven chakra points—energy centers like the heart and genitals. She pointed to a tray of stainless-steel medical tools. The purpose of these instruments is to probe those organs, inflicting the maximum amount of pain while keeping the victim alive for as long as possible. Let's begin."

***

"Jesus, Mary, and Joseph! Californian roads get worse and worse," Jeannie said to an empty passenger seat. *Each year, the gullible voters of this state keep voting for more and more taxes that are supposed to go to improving our roads. Yeah, right!* She decided to spend the night in Arizona. *Pretty good progress for the first day,* she thought. But the roads she drove the next day through New Mexico were just as bad as those in California.

Two cars played leapfrog behind Jeannie at a considerable distance. Only if she had been looking for a tail could she possibly have noticed them. Due to the long stretches of road they were traveling, the two vehicles were in intermittent close proximity. They relayed their route, not knowing Jeannie's final destination other than that she had left California.

The motel was rated on her GPS as a 5-Star. *God, I would hate to see what a 1-Star is like.* She had picked up some fast food and decided to dine in. After setting down her take-in items on a small table and surveying the room, she turned on the television and began relaxing after the long drive. *Holy shit!* Every channel she changed to was basically reporting the same news. Black Cell. *No wonder Sean hasn't called me.* Four men rented two rooms down the hallway from hers.

***

At two in the morning, Sean, half-awake, heard his cell vibrating. The screen showed Akari. "Where are you? I was worried," he said.

"Hello, Agent Delaney. I heard that you are looking for me. I have to admit that Akari did a pretty good job of spying on me." Sean felt his pulse start racing. "It was only recently that I learned from my friends in the area that this bitch was watching me. I am afraid your partner is tied up right now and cannot come to the phone, but she will be here when you arrive. Just trace her cell phone and leave Black Cell alone."

Sean, now wide awake, called headquarters and requested a trace on Akari's phone call. It was easy to trace since it was still activated. Sure enough, it was in the red circle area. Sean felt his chest tighten and his mouth become dry. Repeated calls to her cell went to voice mail. *She wasn't a double agent. How could I have doubted her?*

"Call in the locals. Our Interpol agent needs immediate help," Delaney shouted into his cell as he ran out of the hotel to a parked cab, still buttoning his shirt. He offered the cabbie extra fare if he could get him to the given address in record time.

A uniformed Japanese police officer had already cordoned off the area when they arrived. There were no ambulances or EMT vehicles yet. *Maybe this is a good sign,* he told himself. He tossed money to the cabbie, rushed to the taped barricade, showed his identification, and was allowed to proceed.

A plainclothes officer stopped him from entering the basement room and asked for his name and identification. Sean told him.

"Agent Delaney, you don't want to go in there. She is dead."

"No, I need to see her."

"Sir, she has been partially decorticated."

Delaney looked at him and paused. "What do you mean decorticated."

"I mean, she's been skinned. A method used in the past by Yakuza.

"I'm alright. Please let me enter." Akari was unrecognizable. The metal table holding her body was covered with blood. On a side table lay her heart, breasts, and genitalia. Her fingers had been cut off as well as her toes. He hoped that sometime during the torture, she had died of a heart attack brought on by shock. He left the room and immediately vomited, then became lightheaded as if he were going to pass out. He sat outside until the medical examiner arrived.

Chapter Eighteen

"WHERE HAVE YOU been?" Akio asked when he saw Yuma enter the room with the other hackers.

"I took care of a pest and had some fun at the same time. An Agent Delaney from Interpol is trying to locate us, but we have nothing to worry about. His informant will not be supplying any more information. What is the status here?"

"We have been making generous deposits to deserving non-profits from the Republican and Democratic Party funds we seized last night. Pointing to the hackers in the other room, he continued, "They will have plenty of work to do, so you and I can focus on our next adventure; military Phase Four. Did you cut yourself? There's some blood on the side of your neck."

"It's not mine, so no problem. How do you want to proceed?"

"It is now time to show the world who holds the real true power. While you were absent, we found the back door into several defense departments in China, Russia, and the United States, but I do not want to set off our attack until we can hit China and Russia at the same time. Now that you are here, perhaps we can proceed. I hope to set off our attack on Valentine's Day. I think that would be a nice day, and it gives us plenty of time."

***

Jeannie woke before her alarm went off. It was only 7:15. She checked to see if she had lost an hour due to one of several time changes she would make on her trip to the east coast. *Yep, lost an hour. Probably lose another one going through the northern part of Texas.* She changed her watch and made a mental note to do the same in her car once she left the motel. However, once in the car, she noticed the clock had automatically adjusted to the new time zone.

The motel advertised that they offered complimentary breakfast in the morning, but when she entered the lobby, she was disappointed. Guests were offered stale sweet rolls, milk, coffee, and yogurt. *Nope, since I'm on vacation, a big breakfast is in order.*

She saw road signs announcing a turnoff for a Waffle House restaurant and decided to check it out. Heads turned when the locals saw a bright red 2020 Corvette pull into the parking lot. "What a gorgeous car," the hostess said when Jeannie entered. "I bet it's fast."

"Thank you. And yes, it's fast, that's for sure. Do I need to be seated?"

"Oh, no, hon. Sit wherever you like. Would you like some coffee?"

"That would be great." Jeannie found a table near a corner and sat down. The place was very clean, and the food smelled amazing. *Either that or I'm famished,* she thought. She ordered two waffles, two links of pork sausage, two bacon slices, scrambled eggs, and hash browns. Grits were not offered. She had never eaten grits and could not wait to try them. *Further south, I guess.*

Two men entered and took a seat at the bar. Both looked European, but Jeannie could not be sure. One was wearing a ball cap which he did not remove, blue Levis, and a white with red sleeves baseball shirt. The other wore a pair of tan Dockers and a short-sleeved tan shirt. He had a tattoo on his lower left arm but was too far away for her to see what it was.

While eating, she tried to pick up a change in the accents of fellow diners. *None so far. Sound just like Californians.* While on her second cup of coffee, she checked her Google Map. Not finding what she wanted, she switched over to her Waze app. Unless she found some attractions she wanted to see that weren't too far off the main highway, she thought she could make it to either Oklahoma or Arkansas by evening, but there was no hurry. Although, the more she thought about it, Arkansas might be an unrealistic stretch.

The two men left before she did. She noticed they took two Styrofoam containers with them. *Orders to go?*

***

Back in his hotel room, Delaney was still in shock and overcome with a desire for revenge. The medical examiner had told him that Akari was awake during at least part of the dissection. Somewhere during the ordeal, her heart gave out. That did not stop Yuma from continuing her mayhem. Sean was having a hard time handling her death. Sure, they had been intimate, but what really hurt was remembering her saying that solving this case could be her long-awaited ticket out of Japan. And now, that psychopath had tortured and killed her. *Yuma's day will come*, he thought. *She, too, will experience a slow and painful death.*

Raiding the mini bar in an unsuccessful effort to resolve his remorse, he heard his cellphone ring. It was Jeannie. He reached to answer but then retracted his hand. *No time for you, I'm afraid. Akari must be avenged.* He stopped for a moment. *Maybe I'm also a sociopath. I have a conscience, but it's weak. Sometimes I feel guilt and remorse, but that doesn't stop my behavior. And look at my relationship with Jeannie. I use others as objects for my own benefit.*

He was brought back to the moment when his cell rang a second time. It was HQ. "Sir, this is Delaney… Yes, thank you, sir. She was a great partner…No, I don't know how she ended up where we found her… Yes, I'm calling to request the Americans' help."

***

Back on the road, Jeannie was glad the freeway was better than the roads in California, Arizona, and New Mexico. *Still no answer or recall from Delaney. Either I pissed him off somehow, or he's really involved in this hacking case. Wow, what a well-maintained road. Guess the people's tax money really does go to fixing and maintaining highways down here.* Her thoughts turned to the serial killer case in Idaho. Forgetting the time change and how early it was in Idaho, she placed a call with Sgt. Elders of the Idaho State Police and got his voice messaging system. She told him she would call again around 5:00 p.m. Oklahoma time, hoping he would be in the office then.

Jeannie became lost in thought about the case as she drove. *The police and autopsy reports suggest that the rounds used by the suspect were specially designed for maximum internal damage; they would penetrate but not exit. He wanted everyone to know he hunted his prey. He was an outdoorsman and knew the area. It appeared that with so many remains found in the same area, he knew his victims would run in predictable directions.*

Again, knowledge of the terrain. But how did he lure his victims? Were they also outdoor enthusiasts? Hikers? Did they know him and accompany him willingly to that desolate area? No, that's unlikely. He had to be meeting them somewhere locally and enticing them to get in his car or have them meet him at a specific location.

She wanted desperately to put her random thoughts on a whiteboard to see if any connection would jump out at her. A siren and red and blue lights broke her concentration. *Shit!* She looked at her speedometer. Eighty miles-per-hour.

The trooper got out of his police car and cautiously walked to Jeannie's driver-side window. She thought it was weird to have thoughts of the great Burt Reynolds film, *Smokey and the Bandit*, and that she had just been pulled over by Sheriff Buford T. Justice. Two black SUVs with two men in each whizzed past.

Jeannie had already lowered the window and placed both hands on the top of the steering wheel as she waited for the officer to approach. "Can I see your driver's license and registration?" he asked. Jeannie slowly reached for her purse, but before opening it told the officer she was an FBI agent and that there was a gun inside. She had turned in her service weapon to IA but still had her personal Sig Sauer. She noticed the young patrol officer place his right hand on top of his service pistol. "Let's leave the purse alone for a while. Is your FBI credential also in it?"

Jeannie realized their predicament. She had turned in both her badge and service weapon, but she still had a small badge kept in her wallet. That would verify her law enforcement status, but since the gun was in proximity, there was a danger that the officer would react when he saw it.

"Look, officer, my name is Jeannie Loomis. I'm the Assistant Special Agent in Charge of the San Francisco Bureau. How would it be if I hand you my purse and you remove the weapon and my ID? I realize I was exceeding the speed limit. I was preoccupied thinking about a case I'm working on with the Idaho State Police." *Not to mention that legally, I wasn't supposed to leave California.*

"Idaho's a long way from here, Agent Loomis. Are you following up on a lead?"

"No. Actually, I'm heading to South Carolina to handle my recently deceased aunt's affairs. But, I was running the case through my head and lost track of the speed limit." *OK, that was a little fib. I'd glanced at the speedometer but loved handling the Corvette on smooth roads.* "If you'd like, I can reach over with my left hand and open my purse, and you can see me retrieve my wallet."

"That would be fine."

Her wallet was atop the gun and easily removed. She turned away from her purse and opened her wallet, deliberately allowing the officer to see her FBI badge, then removed her California driver's license and handed it to him. He quickly looked at the picture and then at Jeannie. "Damn, the FBI must pay big bucks to be able to afford such an awesome ride." Jeannie relaxed, already getting the feeling that professional courtesy would prevail.

"No. It's from my inheritance. I recently lost my mom as well. We're only young once."

"True. It's a beautiful car, and we don't see many if any newer model Vettes out here." Handing back her license, he added, "A word of caution, though. A few of my fellow officers out here would love to tag an FBI agent in a Corvette—if you get my drift. So, until you get into the next state, keep it close to the posted speed."

Jeannie thanked the officer and pulled back onto the roadway. *Shit! That'd be all I'd need. A citation for excessive speed, or, for that matter, having my ass hauled in for reckless driving outside California. Slow down, girl, and put the car on cruise control if you're going to daydream.*

Jeannie thought about her life during the remainder of that day's drive; her childhood, her college and university years, her two failed marriages, her reckless former lifestyle, and the loss of her unborn child. With the road generally a long straight ribbon of asphalt, reminiscing about her life and listening to various radio stations and recorded media was about all she could muster. She finished listening to the Ark of the Covenant audiobook and a few CDs and realized it was time for a bathroom stop and some coffee.

Back in the car, she rationalized that she had led a decent life and had survived many ups and downs.

She recalled something her mom often said, "We all have a past, and we all made choices that weren't the best, perhaps. None of us are completely innocent, but we all get a fresh start every day to become a better person than we were the day before."

Great advice, Mom, but why didn't you tell me you had a sister?

Chapter Nineteen

"AGENT DELANEY, I'M Celia Johnson." She did not say what agency she represented, but earlier, his supervisor advised him that a person from the NSA would be contacting him shortly. He assumed she was with the NSA, but she could also have been with the CIA.

"Thank you for your quick response," Sean answered.

"As you requested, we examined a flyover at the location you reported. If you text me your email address, I'll send you the visuals. We did get a plate off a van leaving the building in question, and, aware of your urgency, we ran a record check on it. It was a stolen vehicle, but it has since been found burned and abandoned. I'll send you overviews of that as well. As you'll see, the area is heavily wooded, and by the time our flyby took place, whatever vehicle was used to leave the area was gone or out of sight."

"I see." Delaney processed the information, trying to connect the dots. "Let me ask you this. Is it possible to analyze the flyover areas adjacent to that of the abandoned van? In other words, the woods made it difficult to see that particular area, but could you expand the view to the surrounding terrain?"

"Very interesting. Yes, that can be done. Give me twenty to thirty minutes, and I'll get back to you." Without waiting for confirmation, she hung up.

Delaney knew what had happened. Luckily either an NSA or CIA spy satellite had flown over the areas in question. Johnson needed to go back to what she or her co-workers had done on the death house and van, and scrutinize the surrounding areas, hopefully picking up Yuma's trail.

Sean checked his emails until he received Johnson's return call and requested information. The quality of the flyover photos she sent was excellent. He easily recognized the complex where Akari had been tortured and saw four individuals leaving the building immediately after Yuma had placed the phone call to him using Akari's cell. *Yuma and three others!* Johnson was right about the van's location. At first, Sean could not locate the vehicle, but then he saw smoke rising through the treetops. *Whoever analyzed the video feed focused in on the van, but what good is that now?*

He reviewed the images of the four suspects exiting the building and approaching the van. Again, the analyst had zoomed in, enabling Sean to immediately recognize Yuma. Her image was still on the screen when his cell rang. *Yuma, the burning van's not going to help you!* he thought as he picked up the phone. "Delaney, here."

"Agent Delaney, we may have some good news for you."

***

An abandoned nuclear silo complex remained on the Chinen peninsula in the southern part of Okinawa. The U.S. had secretly stored nuclear weapons there as well as throughout Japan following World War II. Clandestine agreements between the two governments allowed nuclear weapons to remain in Japan until 1972. Now, as in other allied countries, there was no more use for these antiquated facilities. The nuclear missiles were removed, and the buildings were left for the environment to reclaim or sold to survivalists who converted them into shelters.

Akio was typing on his keyboard eighteen stories below the surface. Several large wall-mounted screens facing him had been divided into sub-screens, simultaneously displaying military bases in the U.S., Russia, and China. Another screen displayed the Atlantic, Pacific, and other world oceans. Sitting next to him was Yuma, who had just returned from the bathroom to remove blood smears from her face.

"If we can get all sides to believe an imminent nuclear attack is about to take place and direct all their energy and resources toward that possibility, we can pursue our real objective. As Interpol, the U.S., and other governmental agencies try to locate us, we will continue to be several steps ahead of them."

***

The adjacent area flyovers paid off. A panel truck leaving the quadrant just north of the burning van was clearly visible. It had been driven approximately fifteen miles to what appeared to be an abandoned warehouse, parked behind a building, and concealed from passing traffic.

Three hours later, the Japanese authorities and members of Interpol's response team had the location surrounded. Units in the rear informed Delaney that the truck was no longer there. *Shit! Did they escape again? How could they?* He requested police surveillance of the warehouse while his assault teams organized. They didn't have time to leave. What had Akari said before? "You are in Yakuza territory. Everyone is watching you."

Delaney gave the order, and all units advanced on the complex, but there was no resistance. The building was vacant. Following an extensive search, the area was secured. Black Cell had vanished, and, more importantly, so had Yuma. Revenge would have to wait. The mystery was how they had escaped.

Akari's words again entered Sean's thoughts. *Let's say they were tipped off by Yakuza or a police officer on the take. Who knows?* Delaney didn't give a rat's ass about the money drained from politicians' and social elites' bank accounts. Yes, the world was on the edge of nuclear war and at DEFCON level two, but the immediate situation was personal.

He released the assault teams and remained at the warehouse with a few Interpol agents. "I want this place immediately searched again from top to bottom. Look for anything that might tell us where they went."

Hours passed. A frustrated Delaney asked local agencies and Interpol to start working all their confidential informants. "Push them, intimidate them. Do anything to get the information." Hours passed, and still nothing. About to call an end to the search, the missing piece of the puzzle was found. An agent found a scrap of paper showing a location in Okinawa. Delaney looked at it. *Got you, bitch!*

Chapter Twenty

JEANNIE WAS IMPRESSED with Oklahoma, Georgia, and Alabama. All joking aside and trying not to be judgmental based on the state's well-maintained highways, she found the states beautiful. Green, lush forests flanked both sides of the highways. All the rest areas she used to either relieve herself or just stretch her legs were well managed and clean, and everyone she encountered during the trip was genuinely friendly, not phony like some of the liberals she dealt with in California.

She finally had her first taste of grits and liked it. It was both sweet with butter and sugar and savory with cheese and bacon. The waitress got a kick out of watching her taste it. "Not bad," Jeannie reported. She loved engaging waitresses in conversation and listening to their southern accents. She had never been called "Hon" until her trip south. And every "You come back now" brought a smile to her face. There was no doubt about it; she was in the deep south. Her next culinary adventure would include black-eyed peas and shoofly pie.

She was amazed to find so many fireworks businesses advertised and located along the roadways. *Can't wait to see what the Fourth of July is like down here.*

At her last stop, she bought a sandwich and soda and waited until she pulled into a wooded rest to eat and call Sgt. Elders. Fortunately, there was a vacant and shaded picnic table that offered relief from the relatively high humidity, which, to her surprise, really did not bother her much. While eating, she pulled out a binder in which she had written various thoughts about the case. Finished with the sandwich, she made her call, not noticing two SUVs parked on the other side of the parking lot.

"Agent Loomis, right on time," Sgt. Elders answered.

"Please, call me Jeannie."

"Right. I forgot. Jeannie it is. A lot has transpired since I last talked with you, so let me bring you up to speed. The suspect has been active for a long time. A construction crew clearing another area of plants for 'copters several miles from where the first bodies were found discovered two more human remains. The coroner estimates they have been there for over a year. We also found a necklace on the ground inscribed with the name Cindy McIntosh, a 17-year-old out-of-work secretary who moved to Idaho from Iowa. She had been reported missing for fifteen months." Sgt. Elders paused, letting Jeannie process what he had shared.

"So, if she'd flown directly to Idaho when she left Iowa fifteen months ago, her killing falls in line with the coroner's guess that the bones had been there for at least a year. I'm sorry, go on," Jeannie said, sipping her soda and taking notes.

"Yes, it matches the time frame. Backtracking, we found the victim had taken a job as an exotic dancer to make ends meet. A request was put out to all surrounding jurisdictions for missing person reports as well as checks on bars and clubs. To date, most of those missing have been found. But those who are still unaccountable all worked as exotic dancers, which doesn't look good for them."

"How many are still confirmed missing?"

"Twelve, and who knows how many more there are who've never been reported. All pieces of evidence from the recent find have been sent to the Idaho State Police Lab for analysis. Ballistic tests have come back, and, as you've already guessed, they were all fired from the same high-powered rifle." Elders paused again, and a few seconds of silence passed. He believed he could hear Jeannie writing on a piece of paper, and he was right. Jeannie had been scribbling her thoughts with a series of question marks. *Twelve? This guy has killed more. A lot more. Why did the victims become exotic dancers? Was it simply to make ends meet, as Elders says? Who frequents these places? Locals, truckers? How does the suspect know his victims wouldn't be missed?*

"Sorry, Sergeant, I'm just writing some notes. Go on."

"Here's where it gets interesting. Two days ago, a Paula Baldwin was seen running for her life down a country road in a purple blouse and thong underpants with her hands handcuffed in front. She flagged down the driver of a pickup, and not wanting to go to the police, she asked the truck driver to drop her off at her apartment, which he did. Once inside and more fully dressed, she called us."

"Sounds like you guys got the break you were looking for."

"When the patrol officers arrived at her apartment, she began crying uncontrollably. One of the officers removed her cuffs and tried to calm her down. They both stated that she was very credible and very frightened. I'm sending you her interviewer's zip file now. Maybe you can pick up something we've missed. I agree with the patrol officers; she's legit. OK, I just sent it."

There was a moment of silence while Jeannie waited for the file to show up on her laptop. When it did, she said, "I'm just having lunch. I can view it and get back to you shortly if you'd like?"

"That would be great. Enjoy your lunch."

After disposing of her lunch garbage, she opened the zip file. Paula's video showed a slightly overweight dish-water blonde whose short hair did nothing to hide her acne-scarred face. Holding a Kleenex, she told her story.

She admitted to being a stripper as well as a prostitute to make extra money. On the night of the kidnapping, she was working a side alley and was approached by a wiry male with a scruffy beard. He was white, about six-feet tall, wore glasses, and stuttered when he spoke. He did not seem threatening, so she got into his older model blue four-door sedan.

As soon as she got into the car, he asked her to put on her seatbelt. As she was fastening the belt, he quickly slapped handcuffs on her before she could react, then placed a wooden-handled revolver against the side of her head and told her that if she tried to get others' attention, he would kill her.

They drove for about fifteen minutes through a respectable residential neighborhood, making several right and left turns, until they got close to his destination. He made her bend down before arriving at his house. Once he was in the driveway, he hit a garage door opener attached to his sun visor and drove in. When the garage door was fully closed, he got out of the car and walked around to the passenger door, opened it, and roughly dragged her out, holding on to her cuffed wrists.

The home was well kept, with one wall decorated with hunting trophies. She remembered one being a deer and another an elk. There were no fishing trophies. He escorted her to his den, where a chain hung from the ceiling. Chaining her, he stripped her of her clothing and piled them on the floor next to her. He then began torturing her by squeezing her nipples and inserting various dildos into her vagina.

When she thought it was over, he returned to the room with ice cubes and cigarettes. He seemed to get excited watching her squirm when the hot lighted cigarettes burned her skin and were followed by the coldness of ice cubes. Then the rapes began. Finishing with her, he hung her back up to the ceiling beam and went to a different room, apparently to sleep.

A few hours later, he returned and told her he would be taking her to his cabin in the wilderness. He cautioned her about trying to escape, saying he already had his alibi worked out and that his friends were willing to lie for him. Besides, who would believe a slut?

After a short drive, they arrived at an airport. He placed her face down on the back seat and told her to stay down. He got out of the vehicle and opened the trunk, and then slammed it shut. She waited a few minutes and looked above the front seat to see where he was. They were in a single plane hangar made of aluminum. She saw him on the passenger side wing of a single propellor plane with an open door, putting a rife inside. That is when she saw her chance of escape, her only chance. She opened the rear car door, got out quickly, and began running. That was when she flagged down the pickup truck.

Jeannie paused the recording and glanced down at her notes. From what she had heard and seen, the victim seemed credible. Jeannie looked at her series of bulleted questions she hoped would be answered further during the interview. If not, they needed to be explored.

- Victim appears to be a very structured female scared to death with a story about being taken at gunpoint and held prisoner at a specific location. Can she describe home and take officer there?
- Was a rape kit completed at hospital? Was semen or other biologicals found?
- Can she take officers to the airport? Can she identify the plane if still there?
- If so, who is the registered owner?
- How bad was his speech impediment?

Jeannie stopped, and after a short walk to use the restroom facilities, she returned to the picnic table and called Sgt. Elders to get answers to her questions. Two men playing cards across the parking lot watched.

"Yes, the victim was taken to the county hospital where a complete rape kit was taken, but the victim insisted they go to the airport first to see if the plane were still there. By the way, we're still waiting on the rape kit lab report. Anyway, when they got to the airport, they found the single-prop plane as described. Before they got out of their vehicle, a security guard approached and asked if there were a problem. He provided them with the registered owner and even a license plate and description of the vehicle. It fit the description of the vehicle provided by our victim, and the license plate number confirmed the area she described." Elders paused, giving Jeannie time to write down her thoughts before he continued.

"A two-man unit was sent to the address of the registered owner in hopes of talking with him. No one was home, but before they left, a vehicle matching the description pulled into the driveway."

"So far, it appears that everything your victim has told you is spot on."

"Yes, that's true, but the suspect had his own story to tell. The guy's name is George Arnold. He's a baker here in Coeur d'Alene and was as cool as a cucumber. He calmly invited our officers into his home and answered all their questions."

"He said he was at a friend's house from five-thirty in the morning and that later, he went to the airport to install a new seat in his Cessna. He even gave them consent to search his residence. They found the inside of the home exactly as our victim described it, you know, the mounted animal trophies. But this only proved that she'd been in the house, not that Arnold had tortured or raped her. They couldn't find anything until near the completion of the search."

Jeannie felt her heart race. *They would find the gun and maybe some article that belonged to the victim. Case closed.*

"The officers noticed a loose floorboard in the master bedroom closet and found a collection of weapons underneath. Now, that wasn't surprising since it was obvious that Arnold was an avid hunter. They found a revolver, but it didn't match the description the victim described. The gun, blanket, and the chain she described weren't found on the premises. However, they found two shotguns and a .22 rifle."

"What about the car? Maybe he stashed it there, and what about the plane?"

"No, he gave consent to search the car, and it was clean. Nothing was found to corroborate the victim's story. They went to the airport and searched his plane. Again, nothing. Our investigators contacted his alibis, and they all confirmed his story of the day."

"Damn!" Jeannie said. "I figured you guys had hit the jackpot."

Chapter Twenty-one

DELANEY HAD NEVER been to Okinawa. All his prior visits had been to Tokyo, where he met up with colleagues from Interpol. He admired the beautiful gardens and ponds and how polite the Japanese were. His knowledge of Okinawa came from reading a magazine in the seat pocket in front of him during his long flight. Its population was around 1.5 million. Near the end of WWII, in 1945, the U.S. Army and Marine Corps invaded Okinawa with 185,000 troops. During the raging battles, a third of the civilian population perished. Like other battles where the Japanese were determined to save their sovereign soil, the Japanese had constructed an elaborate system of caves that had long since been abandoned.

In a secret 1960s agreement with the Japanese government, the U.S. installed nineteen nuclear weapons in several Okinawa silos. Some used those same tunnels. As years passed, the silos and tunnels became nothing more than tombs of a forgotten time, except for one.

As soon as Delaney deboarded the plane and tried to orient himself, two Japanese males approached. "Agent Delaney?" one of them asked, both showing their Interpol identifications. Sean nodded, and the three walked to the airport exit. "We believe we know where Yuma's residence is. We have been surveilling a nightclub owned and operated by Yakuza. Last night, Yuma and several other women partied at the bar. We tried to follow her back to her apartment and take her into custody, but we lost them heading to the south side of the island. Two teams of agents scoured the area but no luck. Another team returned to the nightclub hoping that she might return, but she did not."

Delaney looked at one of the agent's maps showing the area where his team lost Yuma. *Where are you? Fool me once, shame on you; fool me twice, shame on me* raced through Sean's head.

"You said you lost Yuma somewhere in this vicinity, correct?" Delaney asked no one in particular.

"Yes. Around here, but as you can see, it is a heavy industrial area, and with the way the streets are laid out, it was impossible to follow her closely without being spotted."

Delaney noticed there were numerous apartment complexes mixed in among the various industrial buildings. “I’m not blaming anyone. Let’s call it a day and meet back here early tomorrow morning.” He did not confide in them that he had formulated a plan and that if it panned out, they might locate Yuma and the Black Cell.”

***

“My fellow hackers. Today is the beginning of a new world order. Not like the ones the elites of the world want to create. No, a new world order that we will control for the betterment of the world. But enough talk of ideology. Let’s proceed.”

A large screen descended from the ceiling. “This is the U.S. Navy’s ComSubPac. Thanks to Hirito, who successfully hacked into their system without their knowledge, we now know the exact location of their submarines.” Akio began clapping his hands and was joined by the other hackers in the room. “What we are viewing here is exactly what the U.S. Navy is viewing in Pearl Harbor and other places. With a flip of a switch, so to speak, we are about to cause a lot of asses to start twitching worldwide. Let the fun begin.” He reached over to his keyboard and hit the command key. A highlighted submarine on the screen blinked twice and then disappeared.

***

In the basement of 1430 Morton St. Bldg. 619 in Pearl Harbor, Hawaii, Steven Michael, Commander of Submarine Force Pacific, received an urgent call. "Sir, the USS Jimmy Carter is missing, and we cannot raise her."

"That's a Los Angeles attack sub, right?"

"Yes, sir. Her last location was here." He pointed with a laser pointer to a location on the large screen. "At 14:06 hours, her signature sighting went dark. We immediately attempted contact, but there was no response."

"Do we have any ASWs (anti-submarine warfare planes) in the area to pick up her nuclear trail?"

"The closest one is 215 miles away, sir."

"Move it into the area. Contact other ships in the area and have them proceed to her last known location. I want all hands on deck. Send an encrypted message to the Department of Defense and advise them of the situation."

***

"As the Germans would say, wunderbar." Akio looked at Yuma with a smile and turned back to his group of hackers. "Phase Three is a success so far. The Americans are panicking. What happened to their submarine? Is it having communication problems? Why are they not corresponding? Did it sink? Were they attacked? Let's have some more fun, shall we?"

Another display, like the previous one, illuminated a side wall. “Let’s give Vladimir Putin some heartburn. Yuma, would you like to do the honors?” Yuma walked to Akio’s keyboard and placed her index finger over the enter key. With a smile, she pressed it and watched a submarine on the wall flash twice and then vanish.

“Excellent. Now, as these two superpowers wrestle with what could have possibly happened to their expensive toys, and before they turn their attention toward each other and the Chinese, we have a bigger issue to explore.

“This, ladies and gentlemen, is the ICBC, The Industrial and Commercial Bank of China. It was established in 1984 and has grown rapidly to become the world's largest bank in terms of assets. Its total value as of yesterday’s close is a staggering $3.47 trillion. I need each of you to attack their technology and get me inside their holdings. A million dollars goes to the first Black Hat who cracks their codes.”

Chapter Twenty-two

"OK, LET ME finish watching the interview, and I'll call you back."

"That would be great, Jeannie, and again, thanks for giving us your take on the case while on vacation."

Jeannie hung up and returned to her notes before continuing to view the file. *Something doesn't smell right. Could the victim be lying and taking out some sort of revenge on this guy? Maybe he was a previous John who stiffed her, and this is her way of getting back at him.*

Glancing at her watch, she thought it was time to continue her drive to Myrtle Beach. She placed the laptop on the passenger seat, plugged the computer's charger into her outlet, and started down the highway. Before examining the interview further, she jotted down another item that needed attention. How solid are the suspect's alibis? Could they have been bought by him, and if so, in exchange for what? Just friendship?

Society has changed, and not for the good, she thought. *A lot of people don't believe in right and wrong anymore, and if they do, society views them as kooks. The new reality is greed. People believe in money, or in the case of politicians, money and power.*

Evening was approaching. The sky was shaded from crimson to ultramarine and then ended with a dark-gray color. Jeannie had already experienced what Oklahomans call a tornadic rainstorm. The car's rapidly flapping wipers were barely able to keep up with the downpour. In between the heaviest rains, she increased her speed down the wet highway, the tires hissing as if telling the rain to give it its best shot. Driving a Corvette, she could ill afford to run into hail stones. The clouds opened. The rain was steady, but the warmth reminded Jeannie of Hawaii. *Got to love the south.*

Another thought ran through her mind. *Why was the suspect so calm, or, as Sgt. Elders claimed, as calm as a cucumber? Hell, if someone came to your house and accused you of rape and kidnapping, your heart should be racing a mile a minute. But that's what usually fucks up an investigation when we try to find a reason for everything.* She reached over, turned on the computer, and returned to the interview, watching it intermittingly while concentrating on her driving, but her primary focus was on the tone of the victim's voice.

***

Sean returned to his hotel room to place a call. "Delaney, how goes it?" SAC Lomax said upon answering. Lomax thought that Delaney was probably going to question him about the Jeannie investigation and was quickly formulating a response that would convey his inability to discuss it. To his surprise, however, Delaney had a request. It was granted, and Lomax transferred his call to Darcy, the San Francisco FBI bureau's tech wiz.

"Agent Delaney, how are you?" Darcy asked.

Delaney immediately got down to his request. "Darcy, as you're aware, a worldwide manhunt is underway to shut down the Black Cell before they can do any more harm. Bloody hell, we have Russia, the U.S., China, and Great Britain waving their nuclear swords at each other. What I'm about to ask was first put to your SAC who approved it, providing it's all kept on the QT."

"I love the intrigue already. Are you aware that U.S., Chinese, and Russian submarines have gone missing? Never mind, what do you need?"

"No, I wasn't aware of missing submarines. My God! I'm going to email you some files showing surveillance shots in a heavily industrialized area of Okinawa. The files were obtained from the NSA, but now I'd like to proceed without their involvement. I can explain later if you must know, but for now, time is not our friend. You'll see a vehicle appear a few times and then disappear. What I'm hoping is that your sources might have conducted a flyover of that area and can tell us where the vehicle went. I'm aware your CIA conducts numerous fly overs, which they deny, but I'm hoping your source might be able to check it out for me."

"Oh, I got it. OK, send it to me and give me an hour or so to get back to you, and I understand that mum's the word."

Delaney thanked her and hung up. It sounded like everything would be kept between the three of them, so he was satisfied. He looked at himself in the hotel mirror and saw the reflection of an unshaven, dark-circled, middle-aged male, badly in need of a shave and shower. *Well, old chap, are we getting closer to solving this case? And once we do, how are you going to end it with Jeannie. She's too nice of a lady for you to be giving her false impressions. You're not the settling down type. You, my friend, are a user. She's strong. She will recover.*

As he was about to begin his room-service dinner, the call came from Darcy. "I have good news for you. A flyover by our friends at Langley did take place during the timeframe in question, and they were able to home in on your vehicle and get its license plate. I'm sending the file to you now. I took the liberty of checking on the registration, but it came back as an offshore company that sounds like another Black Cell rabbit hole. I'll keep peeling back the layers, but I don't think I'll get anywhere. My un-named friends gave me the vehicle's location as of seventeen minutes ago. Here's the location."

***

Delaney put on black trousers, a matching turtleneck sweater, and a black leather jacket. He filled a duffel bag with necessary items and stuffed the address into his waist pocket before going downstairs to the receptionist's desk to order a GPS-equipped rental car. When it arrived, he entered the address and followed the directions to a back-alley apartment about a half-mile from the missile silo. *This has to be the place.*

There was only one streetlight, and it was flickering on and off, ready to die. He remained in the car for ten minutes, hoping that anyone who saw him park would give up on watching what he was doing in the area. Satisfied that no one was watching, he got out of the car with the duffel bag and walked toward the dwelling.

The apartment complex looked like a lot of Japanese high-density housing like where Yuma's mother lived. There were ranks of identical balconies, many displaying similar-looking plants and holding securely locked bikes. Fortunately, the apartment was on the ground floor, and the door did not have a peek-hole that permits a person inside to view their visitor before opening the door. He knew he was in

Yakuza territory, and his only friend was the darkness. He needed to get in and out quickly.

He reached into his front pocket and pulled out a dark nylon stocking he had picked up at a small clothing store near the hotel and pulled it over his head, covering his entire face. He reached across his body with his right hand and pulled out a Sig Sauer 9mm with a suppressor, and knocked on the door, mimicking a coded knock he had seen on numerous television shows. He could hear someone approaching. A lock was released, and the door opened. It was Yuma standing in her panties and a short t-shirt.

Before she could react, he smashed his weapon into her face, knocking her backward, and grabbed her before she hit the floor unconscious. In a catlike motion, he searched the single-bedroom apartment and found no one else.

He looked down at Yuma. There was no movement; she was out cold. He removed the bedspread from the bed and laid it next to her. Then he put his gun back into his shoulder holster. Opening the duffel bag, he pulled out the syringe which he had purchased at a pharmacy for diabetic use and had filled with a liquid substance. Pushing slightly on the plunger to allow some of the substance to squirt out the air bubbles, he bent down, injected the needle into her neck, and emptied its contents. Placing the syringe back in the duffel bag, he rolled Yuma onto the bedspread, and, after rolling her a few times like a rug, he took her motionless body to the trunk of his rental.

Getting into the car, he pulled off the nylon stocking and used the sleeve of his turtleneck to wipe his sweating brow. After running his hand through his matted hair, he started the car and drove to a previously scouted abandoned warehouse. His movement had not been noticed.

***

Jeannie finished watching parts of the interview again and decided to let the new information percolate in her brain for a while before calling Sgt. Elders. As she reached the South Carolina state line, she felt it was time to find a place to stay and call it a day. *No sense in pushing it.* She looked forward to a nice southern dinner and a hot shower. Later, she would review her notes and call Elders. *Sounds like a plan,* she told herself.

Bubba Jim's BBQ restaurant looked like it would fit the bill. As she pulled into the parking lot, she noticed several big rigs parked in the back. Her dad had always told her, "When you see a bunch of truckers at a restaurant, you damn well know it has great food and a lot of it." He was right. She ordered the BBQ sampler plate of pork, sausage, chicken, ribs, and brisket. She skipped the grits and got home fries, corn-on-the-cob, and sweet tea. There was so much food she took the leftovers with her for a nighttime snack once she found a place to stay.

"You all come back now real soon, darling," the waitress said when she paid the bill. She got back to her room and heard her cell activate in her purse. It was Lomax.

"Good morning. Any news on my suspension?"

"Where are you?" he replied.

She quickly formulated a response. "I'm just sitting down for dinner."

"I guess I should have been more specific. What state are you in?"

Shit, busted! she thought.

"Look. Before you yell at me, put yourself in my shoes. I've been suspended on a trumped-up charge. Yes, I'm still getting my paycheck, but it's almost like I was placed on house arrest, just that it was the entire state of California. So, I said fuck'em and took off."

Lomax briefly remained silent, then said. "Jeannie, a federal prosecutor has put out a warrant for your arrest."

"What? What am I being charged with?"

"Flight to avoid prosecution."

"God, it just gets better all the time. How did they know I left the state?"

"I don't know, and I'm calling you from a burner phone. I suggest you also pick one up. After we hang up, I also suggest you think about all the ways they will try to track you and get your ass back to California. Biggest problem I see is that your car that sticks out. When you get back, contact me at this number, and we can come up with a plan to show that you never left this damn state."

Hanging up, Jeannie began to panic. *Why do they want me so badly? Think Jeannie, think. You and Ismail have tracked numerous criminals, how do I cover my track,s and how did they know I left the state? Damn it! I used credit cards for gas, food, and motels. That would be easy to trace, and my God damned cell that I've been using to talk with Detective Elders.*

"OK, the damage has been done," she said to no one. She looked in her wallet and found that she still had the thousand dollars she had withdrawn from her bank. *No more credit cards.* What to do with the car? She used an old-fashioned phone book in her motel room and found what she was looking for. They were still open, so she made a call. About an hour later, a rental car was delivered.

What if they were not tracking me through my credit card use? How else could they know I'm not in California? Opening the Corvette's trunk, she found the pouch that contained roadside emergency equipment and pulled out a flashlight. She found what she was looking for in the right rear fender well; a tracking device. *But who planted the bug? Surely it wasn't the FBI agents who interviewed me. No, it had to be someone whose been following me from day one. Those two black SUVs. It must be the Organization!*

Jeannie found a store that carried burner phones and bought three. As soon as she got back into the rental car, she called the number Lomax had given her. He answered on the second ring. She told him about the tracking device and the two black SUVs and that she now had a rental car paid for with cash. Her plan was to park her Corvette in the parking lot of an Indian casino she passed a few miles back and attach the tracking device to a random vehicle. A taxi would bring her back to the motel.

"It has to be the Organization," she told him. "For whatever reason, they feel a need to track my movements. As for the deputy district attorney who issued the warrant, I'll bet he's part of the Organization as well. Maybe you can check."

"Everything you say adds up," Lomax said. "I'll check out the asshole who issued the warrant. If I can bust him, maybe we can put an end to this nonsense once and for all. Do you have enough money to hold out until you get back? If not, I can arrange to wire you funds. What about your sports car?"

"I'm working on that. And yes, I have enough cash, so I should be OK. I have one last stop to make, and then I'll head back. Talk to you soon."

Those fucking bastards. First, they devise a nice little plan to get my ass back to Austria, then they track my movements. They got an asshole D.A. to issue a warrant for my arrest once they knew I left the state. You want to play games? Bring it on!

Chapter Twenty-three

"Good, you're awake. I can't start the party without you." These were the first words Yuma heard through a splitting headache. As her focus grew sharper, she found herself strapped to a wooden table in a small room made of cinder blocks. She tried fruitlessly to remove her constraints while staring at Delaney wearing a rubber apron, rubber gloves, and eye protection.

"We haven't been formally introduced. My name is Sean Delaney, and I work for Interpol. I had a partner. Her name was Akari. Oh, I see in your eyes that you recall my partner. Bloody shame what happened to her. You see, a sadistic bitch, that's you, tortured her to death."

"Fuck you," she spit back. "I will do the same thing to you, but much slower. Do you know who you are fucking with? I am a member of Yakuza. When they find me, you will experience even more pain than your whore."

"Yes, Yuma. I know who you are, and I know you're also with the Black Cell. Tell me, is Akio your fuck partner? As I said, you're a sadistic bitch who, with Akio Tanaka, think of yourselves as modern-day Robin Hoods, hacking into computers and wreaking havoc on governments and their economies. You now have the superpowers of the world ready to launch nuclear weapons at each other. You consider yourselves geniuses, but you're nothing more than common thieves hung up on your own narcissistic cravings.

"How's Akio? He's next on my list. He thinks of himself as a Messiah, doesn't he? You see, Yuma, you two egomaniacs don't realize there will always be other maniacs in the wings, jockeying to take your positions."

"Fuck you! You don't know shit! You are just another government leech preying on the system. What is this supposed to do, scare me?" She hissed as she pulled on her restraints. "You must follow the law, so your attempt to scare me with all this is bullshit." She again stretched her bindings to exemplify her words while laughing. "Now, take this shit off me, and maybe after I get you alone, I will give you a quick death."

"Yuma," Sean said while shaking his head. "Your first mistake is thinking that I'm here in a law enforcement capacity. No, my fellow colleagues have no idea I tracked you down. As far as they know, we're all still trying to find you and your boyfriend. Your second mistake is thinking I'll be turning you over to authorities so a court of law can adjudicate your case. They would probably say you're insane and send you to a mental hospital for a time. No, Yuma, unless you cooperate with me, I'm afraid there'll be no arrest, and you'll never have a day in court."

"Fuck you! Let me out of here."

Delaney removed a cloth covering a stainless-steel tray. Yuma immediately knew what was coming. There were pliers, various size knives, scissors, a saw, and a plastic bottle of unrecognized fluid. A syringe lay next to it.

"Amazing what a person can buy at a hardware store. Please feel free to scream. No one will hear you but do so if you must. There're so many empty warehouses around here, it wasn't hard to find one that fit my requirements. Shall we begin?"

Not waiting for an answer, he turned his back on Yuma, only to turn and face her again with a pair of surgical scissors in his hand. Silently, he started cutting her t-shirt from the belly button up to the collar, finally removing it from her neck. He then grabbed her underpants and cut both sides, sliding the material off from beneath her. "Such a waste," he said as he turned and put the scissors on the table. "Akio is going to miss this. I need to put a little more juice in your neck to help you cooperate with me.

Now, let's start with an easy one, shall we? Where's Akio and the rest of the Black Cell?"

"Go fuck yourself!" she said before laughing out loud. "You think I will tell you, you shit, you asshole? Untie me, you fuck."

"Sorry, I can't do that. I know that you injected Akari with tetrodotoxin which you got from a pufferfish. Nasty stuff, I understand. It paralyzes the body within ten minutes in some cases. It causes numbness and a sensation of prickling and tingling of the lips and tongue, followed by facial numbness, headache, a sensation of lightness or floating, and profuse sweating. Then comes dizziness, salivation, and nausea.

"Sometimes the person injected has bouts of vomiting, diarrhea, abdominal pain, and difficulty moving their extremities, and they normally lose their ability to speak. You must have refined the poison since Akari spoke to you before you tortured her to death. How am I doing, Yuma? You have much more experience with the substance than I do.

"I also understand from the coroner's investigator that you used a technique called Lingchi. You know, Yuma, that Lingchi is wrongly translated as thousand cuts, and many, like you, believe it started in Japan. No, in fact, it originated in China in about 300 AD. Don't worry, I won't bore you with the history of this torture technique. You'll experience it first-hand."

Yuma followed him with her eyes as he picked up the syringe and extracted solution from the plastic bottle. He turned and looked down at Yuma. Seeing her focus was on the syringe, he smiled. "No, Yuma, I won't be injecting you with pufferfish poison. What fun would it be not to hear you scream? No, this contains hydrochloric acid. I'm forced to use a special glass needle as an injector. See?" He raised the syringe and pointed to the needle at the end.

"Now, chemical burns on your skin can be mild or severe, depending on how much the acid has been diluted and how long it has been in contact with your skin. Oh, you don't have to guess. I didn't dilute the acid for you. Let's try again. Where are Akio and his gang?"

Yuma strained, trying to rise from the table to spit at Delaney. A wad of mucus hit him on his nose. "Oh, I hope you don't have any infectious diseases, but I understand your stress," he said. "OK, let's start with a little between your toes, shall we? Then we can progress to the really painful stuff."

As Delaney tried to spread Yuma's toes, she began to squirm. "That's only going to spread the acid to your other toes," he warned.

"Fuck you!" she yelled. The smell of the acid eating away the area between her little toe filled the room, but Yuma did not scream. She eventually started to answer his questions as the torture increased.

"So, you say Akio is no longer leader of the Black Cell. I assume you now occupy that position?"

"Yes, and the world has not seen anything yet! He said he wanted to steal from the rich and give to the poor. That was all bullshit. Sure, we drained bank accounts and the fuckin' political parties' funds in the U.S. We even got China, Russia, and the U.S. freaked out when their subs seemed to disappear. But if I were in charge back then, we would not have given the money away. It was ours. Those funds and what we would have taken from the bank—we could never have spent all of it in our lifetimes."

"I see. So, it was about the money all along?" She did not answer.

"So, how did you eliminate Akio?"

"Not just him, all of his sexist male pig friends. My girls could out-hack all of them."

"So, it was also competition that did Akio in?"

She laughed. "No, asshole. It was a quick-acting poison that did him in him along with his buddies. My girls will run the Black Cell now."

"Maybe you haven't noticed, but you won't be running anything."

"We will see."

"Now, let's discuss the Black Cell's location, shall we?"

During her torture and somewhere along the road to death, Yuma gave up the silo location and the rudimentary alarm system installed to prevent trespassers. She also helped Delaney visualize the layout of the complex. Later, Delaney drew a crude diagram from memory showing the location of the old missile tube's exterior doors. The main entrance was a heavily guarded tunnel. Another less guarded entrance was through an old elevator shaft that was still operational, according to Yuma. He felt that dismantling the door welds on two of the launch tubes would be a better place to enter. Yuma said they were not alarmed, but of course, he knew she could have lied.

Yuma also said there were several weapons available to the hackers but that her females lacked firearms training and generally were not interested. Hopefully, a show of force after an initial assault would prevent a shootout, but they were Yakuza. Delaney's biggest problem was deciding how he was going to get the information to Interpol without implicating himself and admitting to the tactics he had used to extract the material.

Almost an hour later, Delaney stared at the partially dismembered body on the table. She did not scream much from the acid burns on several areas of her body but began losing it with the removal of her fingers. He wasn't sure when she finally died. He didn't care. More than likely, she died from a heart attack brought on by shock. Hopefully, Akari had died early in the process.

From the far corner of the room, he picked up a gasoline can and poured a generous amount on Yuma's body and his tools, then poured the remaining contents on the floor, allowing it to spread under the torture table. In the adjoining room, he removed his white apron, gloves, and eye protection. Having already placed a five-gallon water bucket in the room near a drain, he stripped off his clothes and poured the water over his head, washing blood down the drain. He subsequently dressed in sweatpants and a shirt and put on a pair of tennis shoes, tossing the removed clothes toward the torture table.

"For you, Akari," he said as he tossed in a lighted pack of matches. The last he heard from the building as he exited was a whooshing sound as fire began to engulf it.

Chapter Twenty-four

AFTER A GREAT night's sleep and a breakfast of waffles, sausage, bacon, two scrambled eggs, hash browns, and several cups of coffee, Jeannie was back on the road, telling herself that it was going to take many workouts to remove the weight she'd put on with just breakfast alone. With what she hoped was only a short stop at the casino where an auto transport company would pick up her car and deliver it to Ismail's house, she should reach Myrtle Beach by early afternoon. She noticed that the car she had transferred the tracking devise to had already left. *Happy tracking, assholes!* She stopped and topped off her gas tank, amazed at how cheap gas was in South Carolina versus the Bay area.

Making good time, she realized her burner phone was vibrating. "Hey, Ace. How's it going?" She could see on the screen that it was Ismail Flores.

"You're not getting too comfortable in my office, are you?"

"You're office. Hell, I've already had maintenance put my name on the door, and you'll love what I've done with the place. Hot tub, 77" LG television with surround sound."

Jeannie laughed. "Yeah, right. If you did that, Lomax would die of a heart attack after he killed you. Working any interesting cases?"

"Never mind me. I heard those fuckers put out an arrest warrant on you. If we had a fuckin' president with balls, this shit wouldn't be happening. Are you keeping a low profile? Do you need my help?"

"Since you ask, yes, I need you to do me a favor."

***

Jeannie found a local non-religious station on the radio featuring old-time rock-n-roll but turned it off so she could concentrate. *Have I covered my tracks the best I can? I haven't seen the two black SUVs for a while. Hopefully, they're heading toward New York or Florida. I've been paying cash for everything, including the car transport company. No paper trail there. Can I resolve my aunt's estate and get back to California without being caught? That's the big question I now face.*

Her burner phone rang again. It was Lomax. "Do you have a weapon?" he asked.

"Yes, my backup; why?"

"I don't know if you've thought about it, but if the Organization feels they might lose the opportunity to force your return to Austria, well..." His voice hung in the air.

They might just kill me!"

She pulled into a Subway and ordered a sandwich, scanning the parking lot for a tail. Lomax's words echoed in her head. Being 11:15 a.m., Jeannie found a vacant back booth to herself, giving her a full view of the parking lot. She ordered a refill of sweet tea and prepared to call Sgt. Elders. Her notes lay before her, and with pen in hand, she made the call, trying to suppress her thoughts of the Organization. She could tell something was wrong by the sound of Elders' voice when he answered the phone.

"Jeannie, I need to tell you that our investigation into the rape and kidnapping of our victim has been closed, effective late yesterday afternoon. I mean, I've been ordered to close the matter. It's no longer an active case. The homicides are still being investigated, but we've been told to forget about Arnold."

"What? What do you mean it's no longer active? The last time we talked, I felt you were close to putting the noose around that son-of-a-bitch's neck."

"Jeannie. Give me fifteen minutes, and I'll call you back when I'm away from the station. Is that OK with you?"

All during the lunch rush, Jeannie's head was spinning over what she had learned in the return phone call. Sgt. Elders had been ordered to close the Arnold investigation. The victim had been shown a photo line-up in which she quickly picked Arnold as her rapist and kidnapper. But then, unbelievably to Jeannie, the case began to unravel.

Hoping to solidify their case in the absence of hard evidence, the victim was asked to take a polygraph. She refused. Her occupation gave her an inherent fear of the police. This, in turn, gave the police an inherent distrust of her.

"You see, Jeannie, in the last election, the dumb shits up here elected an extreme left-wing district attorney. He believes the root cause of all crime is the lack of proper redistribution of wealth. He lives in a different game of Monopoly where if a person lands on someone else's piece of property, it's OK to loot and burn if you desire. You know, the new world order and such. Our chief is nearing retirement and doesn't want to make waves on his way out, so he isn't challenging the DA's refusal to prosecute the case."

"Yeah, we have a similar situation in San Francisco, at least the locals do," she said. "Fortunately, our cases go through the federal system, but that's getting more and more liberal too. It's getting so bad that San Francisco is the number one city people are moving from, so don't get me started. So, are you working the case on your own?"

"Yes. I'd probably be suspended or fired if the chief knew I was carrying on the investigation. I mean,

I'm still handling my caseload, but any chance I get, including when I'm off duty, I'm going to work this case. I know he did it."

Sounds like me. Unofficially helping Idaho with a federal warrant out for my arrest, Jeannie thought to herself. "OK, your secret's safe with me. So, let's continue. You said she was offered the opportunity to take a polygraph test, but she refused due to her distrust of the police. I can see that. Go on."

"Well, that, and the fact that we couldn't get any hard evidence to corroborate her story of disappearance and reappearance. Of course, her lifestyle left a lot to be desired. All that led to the case being deactivated."

"But do you believe her story?" Jeannie asked.

"Absolutely, and because of this, I'm not letting go. The fact that Arnold was going to transport our victim by plane intrigued me. He was going to fly her out, but where to?"

Jeannie looked at her notes, and about halfway down the page, she saw that she had written the same question. "I believe there are too many details for the victim to have fabricated the story. I found that Arnold had moved from Cedar Rapids, Iowa, to Idaho about thirteen years ago. I don't know if I told you before, but he opened a bakery on the outskirts of town about three miles from his home. The bakery became a huge success, and you can imagine the number of cops stopping by for a donut. Personally, I've never been there. Of course, a lot of them took his side in the investigation, saying it was a bunch of shit coming from a whore."

"Arnold is married, and they have two children. Apart from his stuttering problem, he instantly blends into his surroundings when he arrives in the Coeur d'Alene area. When not working at the bakery, he enjoys flying and hunting. It all adds up."

"Sounds like it to me. You just need a few more items, and you should be able to wrap this asshole up. I can't believe your chief called it quits. Do you think if I called him, maybe I could convince him to reopen it?"

"Oh, God, no, Jeannie! Please don't. He'd bust a gasket knowing I contacted the FBI after being told to back off Arnold. At a minimum, I'd be suspended."

"Let me ask you this, and don't worry; I won't contact your chief. Have there been any fresh kills that you're aware of?" Jeannie asked.

"No, and that's the other thing. Since we searched his house and interviewed him, we haven't had any new missing persons. I know this doesn't mean there aren't other bodies that he dumped and buried in the wildness, but the killer seems to be inactive."

"Well, the killings may have stopped since you put the heat on him, but believe me, his urge to kill is increasing each day. He can't shut it off."

Chapter Twenty-five

Delaney's cellphone vibrated on the nightstand. He had already been awake for several hours trying to think of the best way to send the information he forced out of Yuma to headquarters. Having decided, he found an all-night internet café on the outskirts of Okinawa, and from there, he sent an anonymous email to Interpol giving the Black Cell's location and other valuable insights about their holdup. Then he waited.

The phone rang several times before he answered. "Delaney."

"Agent Delaney, this is Helen at HQ. We got a location for the Black Cell. The director is on the other line and wishes to talk with you. Shall I connect?"

Two hours later, Delaney was in the police station closest to the abandoned missile silo complex. In addition to Delaney, there were four other Interpol agents and six heavily armed and armored SWAT officers. Two undercover officers posing as boyfriend and girlfriend walked past the abandoned weapons facility and noted the exact location of the missile launch hatches along with how they had been welded shut years earlier. Given the years of saltwater exposure and accumulated rust, the welds did not appear to be much of a problem for the assault team. The assault would take place at 23:00 hours.

Delaney requested another flyover by Darcy's "friends" at 22:50 hours to check on possible activity. Darcy promised it could and would be done. The assault teams arrived in three black vans. Delaney led team one consisting of an officer with a cutting torch and two Interpol agents. Another officer with team two had a torch and along with team three, went to the last launch tube hatch. Launch tube number two would not be attacked.

Even by what little could be seen in the dark before the torch was lit, Delaney was amazed at the size of the launch tube door. In less than six minutes, the welds on both tubes had been breached. It took several men to open the hatches. According to Yuma, the launch tubes were far away from the Black Cell's sleeping and working quarters, but Delaney ordered silence, just in case.

With night-vision activated, repelling ropes were dropped, and the three teams began their descent into the darkness. The walls were damp, and the entire area smelled of mold. After what seemed like forever to Delaney, the teams finally reached the bottom of the cavernous tubes. Teams two and three searched the rear of the complex where Yuma said the remains of Akio and the male hackers were held. Delaney and team one waited at the base of launch tube one, covering their flank.

"Team one, this is team three."

"Go ahead, team three."

"Just as the anonymous source reported, there are seven male bodies lying on the floor. Smells pretty bad back here. Met no resistance. We're returning to your position."

Once regrouped, they headed to the main complex. They tried to be quiet, as Delaney had asked, but the sloshing of water around their feet was hard to avoid.

For some reason, Delaney's thoughts turned to the Fuhrer's bunker in Berlin. He had been fascinated by the underground structure as a kid and loved seeing pictures of the place both before and after Hitler's suicide. He had only recently seen a documentary made by someone who snuck into the bunker while the German government was demolishing it. Breaking the law, the photographer entered many of the still-standing rooms and took pictures of what the place looked like after numerous explosives had been set off in hopes of demolishing the walls but having little effect on the heavily constructed complex. The

German government finally gave up and just buried the whole facility, turning the surface into a parking lot. *I wonder why the Japanese government has never done the same, especially with the value of real estate here.*

Yuma said there was only one sentry around the first bend before entering the main complex where the Black Cell members ate, slept, and played at their computers. Delaney spotted her. A single female playing on what appeared to be a handheld video game or perhaps a cellphone. An assault rifle was slung from a shoulder strap, but her hands were not on the weapon.

She obviously sensed something because she removed her earpieces and grabbed the rifle, looking in the direction of Delaney and the assault teams. Apparently, hearing the water sloshing, she yelled out something that could not be heard above the sound of her rifle shots.

The muzzle flash from her automatic weapon gave up her position; she looked like a typical target silhouette. Delaney and the officer to his right returned fire, hitting her numerous times. The thunderous sounds of gunfire echoed throughout the cavernous complex. Gunsmoke filled the air. They quickly passed over her body as their advance picked up the pace. They knew the rest of the Black Cell had surely been awakened.

Reaching the fully illuminated main complex, they faced seven females who had begun firing. Several had automatic rifles, probably AKs, Delaney thought, while two others had shotguns. Rounds ricocheting off the complex walls. Having no barricades to give them cover, they just stood, firing randomly. The gun battle lasted but a few minutes; the seven females lay dead where they had taken position.

Delaney was hit in the shoulder, just above his bulletproof vest. Another Interpol agent took one in the leg, but it did not appear to have hit an artery. None of the others were injured, which was remarkable given the amount of automatic gunfire.

Team two reached the main tunnel entrance that led to the eighteen-story elevator. "Team two, make sure they,"......BOOM. The entire underground area shook from the explosion. "Yuma, you lying bitch!" Delaney screamed as he and the other team members ran to the elevator entrance. Thick smoke filled the area, almost like a dense fog. They nearly stumbled over two Interpol agents, both dead. The elevator and shaft were demolished. "Shit! Shit! I should have guessed," Delaney said as he walked away from the destruction.

Using a satellite phone, Delaney notified his supervisor about losing two agents and requested medical personnel and a forensic team to process computers and related equipment. Everyone would need to use the same two missile silo tubes used during the team's assault. He had snapped a few pictures of the large display in the Black Cell headquarters that showed worldwide submarines' positioning. Delaney sent them to headquarters so that each country's DEFCON could be restored to a less than nuclear confrontation status.

As the assault teams were preparing to be replaced by Interpol agents, local law enforcement, and medical staff and to vacate the silo, Delaney took a walk back past the launch tubes to the end of the complex. The smell told him he was getting close. Bodies were lying flat on the ground. It probably took all the females' energy to drag their former Black Cell male colleagues to their place of rest.

Among the dead, Delaney spotted Akio, as described by Yuma. Mixed in the smell of death was the faint odor of almonds. Yuma must have used an arsenic derivative to eliminate her former Cell members. *Another megalomanic has bitten the dust. The Black Cell is no more.*

Chapter Twenty-six

BY THE TIME Jeannie reached her reservation at the Surfside Beach Holiday Inn, she was fuming about her conversation with Elders and the fact that Arnold, a serial killer, was still free and likely to kill again. *It's only a matter of time*, she thought.

Eating a combination pizza she had picked up from the Mellow Mushroom Pizzeria next door, Jeannie began rewriting her notes. She also added action items, although she was not sure for what purpose.

- To date, a total of twenty-two bodies have been discovered
- Body dumps in wilderness not easily accessible
- Victims - prostitutes, runaways, no one looking for them
- Suspect profile:

- Suspect Arnold – family man, businessman, local
- Criminal history consistent with profile (kidnapping, sexual assault)
- Pilot
- Hunter--knows area--in good shape physically
- Victim positively identifies Arnold

Looking at her bullet points, Jeannie said, "Not much!" out loud to herself. She continued.

- Why the district attorney's reluctancy to file? Elders and his department have enough for a circumstantial case against Arnold. Enough to secure numerous search warrants, at least.

The district attorney told Elders he did not have enough evidence, and the suggestion of getting another consent search brought laughter. The DA told Elders in no uncertain terms that he still lacked hard evidence, pointing out that all the police knew was that twenty-two women had been killed by a maniac, and their bodies had been dumped in the Idaho wilderness.

"Goddamn liberal D.A. I'll bet if one of those victims was his daughter, he wouldn't hesitate to go after the son-of-a-bitch." Realizing she was speaking aloud to herself in a hotel room, she grabbed another slice of pizza and ate. She put the remainder of the pizza in the room's small refrigerator and took a hot shower, hoping to get kinks out of her back. When done, she called Ismail.

"Gee, two phone calls in one day. Miss me, huh?" Ismail asked, answering the second ring. "They haven't arrested your ass yet?"

"Yeah, buddy. I have to admit I miss you too. And no, I'm still on the lamb. Look, I need you to do something else for me, or maybe have Darcy or Burk do it. I want you to send a request to the Cedar Rapids PD in Iowa. I'm sorry to ask you. I don't want to get you in trouble."

"Iowa? There's nothing but corn there. Well, sometimes they do have a pretty good college football team."

"Are you listening?" Not waiting for an answer, Jeannie continued. "Have them go back fifteen years and see what kind of a missing women list they have, probably prostitutes or society castoffs. Also, see how many bodies they've located in their untamed areas prior to fifteen years ago. The key is fifteen years, nothing more recent than that. Got it?"

"Gee, I thought you were on vacation?"

"Very funny, Izzy. Just do it and put a little heat on them. They're going to bitch, whine and complain, so use your charm. You keep telling me you have tons of it, so now's the time to turn it on."

"Well yeah, I do. I guess I can pull myself away from this stressful job of Assistant Special Agent in Charge and do this for you. You know you'll owe me big time when you get back."

"No, you'll owe me big time for allowing you the privilege of being my assistant. Thanks, buddy. Call me at this number, not my personal cell, when you get something back from them. Oh, and say hi to your better half." She realized she was smiling after getting off the phone with Ismail. Arnold had to have started his killing spree in Cedar Rapids. *Why didn't I think about that when Elders told me where he'd lived before coming to Idaho? I bet when this animal is finally nailed, we'll find that as a child, Arnold was into arson and animal cruelty. This might be the break we need to put this bastard away.*

Her thoughts finally turned away from Arnold to what she hoped to learn from her aunt's attorney, with whom she would meet the next morning. She might be able to stay without discovery for another day or two. Her personal car was on the way back to California. A lot depended on what she learned from the attorney and the safe-deposit box contents. *How could my parents have kept this from me?* she again wondered.

***

Delaney's flight back to headquarters in Lyon, France was uneventful. With his arm in a sling, it was not a comfortable flight, but the pain pills helped. He was so exhausted that if any babies had been crying, he had not heard them. He had given the flight attendant instructions not to wake him for the food and beverage service, and now, with one more hour of flight time, he had awakened famished. A flight attendant told him he had awakened just in time for the final beverage rounds, and when asked if there were anything to eat, she told him she would sneak a roll with his tea.

Upon deplaning, clearing customs, and locating his luggage, he went to the food court area and ordered the largest breakfast offered, with yet another cup of tea. His transport could wait awhile before he exited the airport. It was the least Interpol could do for the job he had done.

They traveled in a downpour on the way to headquarters. He was grateful upon arrival that only a heavy mist greeted him. Entering the director's reception area, he was told to enter the office; he was expected. The director rose when Sean entered the room. His warm greeting and accolades culminated in "Job well done!"

"Please, Sean, have a seat. How's the arm?" Clearing his voice and not waiting for an answer, the director leaned forward in his chair. "Because of your brilliant investigation with the Black Cell, I want to give you the opportunity to choose whatever Interpol branch you would like to direct. That is the least our organization can do for you. I remember once when you were offered a plaque, you respectively declined, stating that the plaque would be on a wall that no one would read, and upon the recipient's passing, it would become a burden to his loved ones. What do they do with the damn thing?"

"Yes, I recall saying that, and my belief on the subject remains," Sean responded with a sharp smile on his face.

"That's what I thought—thus, the offer of any Interpol branch you choose. I don't need an answer immediately. Instead, I want you to take at least two weeks off. You've jolly well earned it. Yes, take two or three weeks off, and when you return, you can give me your answer."

Chapter Twenty-seven

THE DRIVE TO attorney Goldstein's office was interesting. She had never seen so many miniature golf establishes on the same street, some right next to each other. Each had its own theme: Jurassic, Pirates, Shark-land, you name it. There were fireworks shops, discount summer clothing stores, bumper water-boat rides, sky-wheel, and various sized roller-coasters.

She saw numerous high risers in the distance and learned that they were now rented by tourists called "snowbirds," the name given to those who flee wintery northeastern states for the warmth of Myrtle Beach. Mammoth resorts sporting names like Grand Cayman, Coral Beach, Compass Cove, and Grand Atlantic offered patrons ocean view condos, multiple indoor and outdoor swimming pools, and moving-water pools called lazy rivers. But the warm ocean water, white sand beaches, and cool breezes that made the humidity bearable were the main attractions.

***

Jeannie found the attorney's office. She parked her car and entered a small reception room, and was immediately greeted by an older woman. After giving her name, the receptionist pushed a buzzer, and Goldstein entered.

"Ms. Loomis, how good it is to meet you in person. Please, come in," Mr. Goldstein said as he escorted Jeannie into his corner office. He was bald and slightly obese but wore a suit that must have cost two thousand dollars by Jeannie's estimate.

"How was your trip? Nice flight?"

"First, please call me Jeannie, and I didn't fly. I decided to take some vacation time and drove here."

"Wow! All the way from California? That's amazing. How long did it take you?"

"Five days, in total."

"So, how do you like Myrtle Beach so far?"

"I've only seen glimpses of the ocean, but no alligators. But I have had grits and sweet tea!"

Goldstein laughed. "I don't think you'll see any alligators down here. You have to go up to Huntington Beach State Park in Murrell's Inlet to see them. Oh, sometimes one shows up in a new subdivision that abuts a pond or lake, but they're usually young juvenile males thrown out of the nest by an alpha male. Once they're seen, the homeowners' associations notify the authorities, and the juveniles are rounded up and either taken to a preserve or to an alligator park then the owners turn around and charge you to see them. How about the Boardwalk or Ocean Blvd?"

"Afraid not. Like I said, I just got here yesterday afternoon, checked into my hotel, and here I am."

"Where are you staying?"

"The Holiday Inn at Surfside Beach."

"I see. Well, I'll be giving you the keys to your aunt's estate, and since no one lives there other than her cat, perhaps you might want to stay there."

"That's a thought. Maybe we can get started? Like I said, this has all come as a shock--learning that I had an aunt." A thought suddenly came to her: *If I stay at my aunt's house, I will be hard to find.*

"Yes, of course. Would you like some coffee while we proceed?"

"That would be great. The coffee at the hotel left a lot to be desired."

Goldstein returned with a tray holding a carafe of coffee, sugar, and sugar substitute, along with a bottle of Cremora and two cups that looked to be china. He poured coffee for Jeannie and himself, and once they had their first sip, he slid open a door of a cabinet behind him and pulled out an accordion-style file. Placing it on his desk, he began taking items out of it.

"As I said on the phone, your aunt was a very wealthy woman. I had the privilege of meeting with her many times over the years after her husband died, your uncle, I guess. We met more often as she advanced in age."

"What did she die of?" Jeannie asked.

"Stroke is what her doctors signed on the death certificate. She'd had a series of what they call TIAs."

"Yes, I'm familiar with the term. My mother had them before she passed. Did she get the Covid shot?"

"Oh, gee, I don't know. Her maid, Isabel, found her sitting in her favorite chair in her garden room. That's the same maid who's been taking care of her cat. Don't remember what her name is. The Sheriff's department found my business card among her phone listings, and that's how I heard of her passing. She could be the sweetest thing at times, but boy, if you riled her, watch out. Her southern charm could turn into a hurricane this quick," he said, snapping his fingers. "God help you if she thought you were lying to or cheating her." He paused for a minute, lost in thought.

Huh! Did this guy try some shenanigans with my aunt, and she caught him? Nah, I think my aunt would've terminated their relationship. Two-thousand-dollar suit. Probably drives a very expensive car. Not sure how to read him. Time will tell.

"Let's see, where were we. Here's the deed to her house. You can't miss it. It's the large house on the largest lot on Ocean Blvd. Drive past all those high-rises, and you'll run right into it. Wait until you see her million-dollar view of the ocean. She and your uncle oversaw the entire building, you know. Sadly, he only got to live in it a few years before he died.

"There is no mortgage on the house. I'm not a CPA or tax consultant, so you'll have to check with one to see if there are any tax liabilities you might have to face. I think you should be OK. Now, there's the cat situation. As I said, Isabel—oh, here it is. This is the name, address, and phone number for her." He unfolded a piece of paper from the binder. Now, here are the keys to the house. Your aunt didn't have a vehicle, so we don't have to worry about that.

"Well, I guess what we have left is the reading of the will. Would you like another cup of coffee before I start?"

"Yes, but first, can I use the bathroom?"

When she returned, Goldstein had already poured her a second cup of coffee. She added some Equal and Cremora.

When Jeannie left Goldstein's office, she could hardly remember where she parked her car. He informed her that she had inherited a fortune and that her aunt had left a complete explanation for her secrecy in a safe-deposit box for which Jeannie now possessed the key. He provided her with a power of attorney that gave her access to the box. He had already called the bank and talked with the bank president, informing him to expect Jeannie's arrival.

Even though she was hungry, she ignored her stomach growling and followed her GPS to the Bank of America listed on the paperwork Goldstein had given her. The house would have to wait until the next day. *Sorry cat.*

She found The Bank of America. It was located on a smaller lot than Jeannie's "B of A" in Newark. "Hello, may I help you?" a very young and attractive black woman carrying a tablet asked Jeannie as she entered.

"Yes, I'm here to get the contents from my deceased aunt's safe-deposit box."

"Do you have an appointment?"

"No. Do I need an appointment to get to a safe-deposit box?"

"Can I help you?" asked an approaching older woman, probably the branch manager.

"Hi. I've just driven over 3,000 miles from the wacko state of California to take care of my recently deceased aunt's estate. She had a safe-deposit box here at your branch. Here's the paperwork from her estate attorney granting me legal access to the box, eliminating any liability to the bank. I hope this clarifies the matter?"

"Oh, I'm sorry for your loss, Ms. Loomis, is it? Can I see the document you have?" Jeannie handed it to her and granted the request to make a copy. "Please, come with me," the assistant manager said, escorting Jeannie to the vault. "Again, let me apologize for the delay. Your aunt's attorney did call our branch manager, and everything is fine." After Jeannie and the assistant manager inserted their respective keys, the box was removed and placed on a table.

"I'll give you some privacy. Just let me know when you're through."

Chapter Twenty-eight

DELANEY HAD SO many emotions and thoughts running through his mind that he decided to visit the hotel bar before going to his room. He spread his trench coat on a chair opposite him, allowing it to dry. The bar was empty except for the bartender who took his order. Sean didn't notice a male enter the bar, eventually becoming aware of him sitting on a bar stool nursing what appeared to be a Manhattan. Sean felt he looked familiar, but he couldn't place him.

A lot of decisions to make, old man, Sean thought to himself. He was getting tired of the commute and general crap associated with Interpol's San Francisco office, thinking it would be nice to be back in Great Britain, but offices in Europe, highly prized by his associates, would be a nice change. *And what about Jeannie?* He realized for the first time that during the whole Black Cell affair, he had not only neglected to call her but that she was not in his thoughts. *Huh!*

He noticed movement out of the corner of his eye as the other customer approached him. He was a clean-shaven Caucasian dressed in casual business attire, about Delaney's height and weight but possibly a little younger. He walked with the air of confidence of a man in control. Reaching out his hand, he spoke.

"Agent Delaney, let me congratulate you on a superb job with Black Cell. The world was on the verge of war until you put an end to it. The President of the United States was shitting his pants, both figuratively and literally. Sorry the explosion blew up a lot of the technology they were using, but what survived is very impressive."

Delaney stared at him and slowly extended his hand. He then realized he had seen the person a few days earlier, also at a hotel bar, an American with no detectable accent.

"I'm sorry, you have me at a disadvantage. Have we met before?" Delaney asked, watching closely as to where the individual had his hands.

"May I?" the male asked, motioning to an empty seat near Delaney's drying jacket. Without waiting for an answer, he sat down and gestured to the bartender to bring more drinks for himself and Delaney.

"Agent Delaney, or can I call you Sean? My name is Mr. Brown. You've served your country well and with distinction. Your work with British Special Forces and

Interpol has been exemplary, including some of your black ops, your 'off-the-book' activities that Interpol is supposedly banned from doing. And, before the Black Cell investigation, successfully terminating Dr. Hausser and his nest of modern-day Nazis. Although I guess we need to share some of the credit with FBI Special Agent Jeannie Loomis, no? How is she, by the way? I understand the Austrian government and the Organization are not happy with her."

"Seems like today is my day to receive praise, but let's cut to the chase, shall we? Who are you with, Mr. Brown? CIA, MI-6, NSA, OGA, some other three-letter agency?"

"All in good time, Sean. Can I pose a hypothetical to you?" Sean did not answer. "What would you do if you could not legally bring the leaders of the Black Cell to justice?'

"What do you mean?"

"I mean, you know in your soul that Akio was the Black Cell mastermind along with his witch of an associate, Yuma, but you had no hard evidence. Nothing to present to a magistrate to get an arrest warrant. Or, better yet, you were able to arrest Akio and Yuma, but some technicality got them off the hook, and they "walked," as we say in America. What would you personally do?"

"I'd use extreme prejudice," Delaney said with no hesitation. "Discreetly, of course, but I'd terminate them." The statement lingered in silence as they locked eyes with each other for several seconds. Delaney felt he was providing the correct response, but still, there was no trust developing between him and Mr. Brown or whoever he was.

"This could either be a relatively short conversation or a conversation that'll change your life forever. What I'm about to tell you is top secret. Leaking this information will result in incarceration for the rest of our lives. Do I make myself clear? If you say yes, I'll ask if you want me to proceed. If you say no, not a problem, I'll leave, and this meeting between you and me never took place. Do you understand?"

Bloody hell. What kind of shit did I get myself into? Delaney's thought as his head began to spin. Did this have anything to do with what he did to Yuma! *Think, Delaney. Could they have found anything to link me to her death? Or was it something else I did in the Army?*

"Would you like me to proceed, Agent Delaney?"

"Sounds like a damned if I do, damned if I don't scenario. If I say no, I'll forever wonder why you contacted me and what you were going to say, while a yes locks me into something that sounds exciting, dangerous, yet ominous." Silence once again filled the bar, only interrupted by the bartender rattling glasses.

"Yes, I'd like you to proceed, and I understand the ramifications of any breach of confidence on my part."

"Great. The organization I head, not to be confused with the modern-day Nazis Organization, doesn't exist and won't be found listed as a black op or off-the-book syndicate. Besides, who would have such a list? The nature of our missions makes it top-secret."

"Does this organization have a name, if I might ask?"

"Special Service Branch."

Delaney raised both of his hands, indicating that Mr. Brown controlled the conversation. Brown continued, "Members of the Special Service Branch conduct strategic problem solving for world governments on the same page. Sometimes, this alliance is a little gray, but overall, the countries that hire us are looking for a better world. No, I'm not talking about the NWO, the New World Order." He laughed slightly and took another sip of his drink. "In fact, many of the problems we solve have a negative impact on the NWO. Shall I continue?"

"So, in essence, you're an organization of problem solvers? And if I can be so bold, the problems you resolve are permanently eliminated?"

"Yes. With extreme prejudice. But, as you know, you eliminate one bad guy, and another one appears."

"You know, Mr. Brown. I have a friend in the FBI who likes to tease me about my name and British accent, to the point of referring to me as the famous fictional James Bond character. What you're faintly revealing sounds very similar to the work 007 was involved in, as created by Ian Fleming."

Mr. Brown nodded. "Would you like another drink, Sean?" Sean accepted, wondering why he was not feeling the effect of the alcohol. *Must be the adrenaline.* After the drinks were delivered, Mr. Brown continued.

"You raise an interesting comparison, and yes, I've heard it. In the Ian Fleming novels, loosely adapted to the big screen, I might add, Mr. Bond worked for the British Secret Service. As I said, we do not. From there, however, there are similarities. We're an organization that performs assassinations worldwide. And, like Mr. Bond, the kills are sanctioned. Should you decide to join our Special Service Branch, your current life would cease to exist. There'd be no time for any long-term relationships. You'd not have a permanent residence. Sean Delaney would simply become a ghost."

Chapter Twenty-nine

THE SAFE-DEPOSIT BOX measured 10" by 10" and was heavy when Jeannie slid it out of the vault. Opening the lid, she saw several beautiful pieces of jewelry heavily encrusted with diamonds, rubies, and sapphires, along with an envelope that had been stuffed with hundred-dollar bills. *Way to go, auntie!* There were also documents dealing with stocks and bonds, things Jeannie would review later.

Not wasting time, Jeannie began transferring the contents to her briefcase. At the bottom was a sealed business envelope that simply had "Jeannie" written on the front. *Must be the letter.* This, she placed in her purse. Leaving the box open on the table, she left the safe-deposit vault, thanked the assistant manager, and informed her the box would no longer be needed.

After signing a document to that effect, she turned in her key and left.

Returning to her hotel room with dinner for the evening, she propped the letter up against the desk lamp. After laying out her meal, Jeannie took the letter and realized by its bulk that it was not going to be light reading. She carefully tore the envelope flap and opened it. Inside were several folded, handwritten pieces of paper. Jeannie had to bend them several times to get them to lay semi-flat on the desk. Pulling the desk lamp closer, she began to read.

> My dear loving Jeannie. If you are reading this, then the chances of me holding you in my arms have passed. How I longed to hold you, smell your hair, look into your eyes. My dearest Jeannie. I don't know you, and you don't know me, but we are one and the same. I have felt the need to write these letters to you over the last forty years to let you know, when you read them, that I have never failed to love you, even if it were from afar.
>
> As you read this letter, I hope God gives you the courage and strength to handle what I am about to tell you and that someday, you will forgive me. You were put on this earth for a reason. You are a miracle from God.
>
> It is hard for me to believe you have grown into a beautiful woman in her forties. Where

have all the years gone? It seems like yesterday that the nurse placed you in my arms. You see, Jeannie. I am your mother.

Jeannie felt her heart race and dropped the paper on the desk, avoiding the emptied food cartons. With tears in her eyes, she picked up the paper and read the final sentence, "I am your biological mother," over and over again.

"No!" Jeannie shouted as she stood, knocking over the chair. She grabbed her purse and ran out of the room. Practically running down the hallway, she pushed open the exit door and made it to her car. Her eyes burned from mascara as it ran from her eyes to her chin. She heard herself again scream "No!" before she started the car and drove out of the parking lot with no destination in mind.

When she awakened the following morning, she panicked. She could feel the presence of someone lying next to her and that she was nude. She felt moisture between her legs. Her head was spinning with one of the worst headaches she could remember. She knew what had happened without the specific details. She thought she had recovered from the destructive lifestyle she had led before she learned she was pregnant. She had sworn off alcohol. She was going to the gym regularly to get in shape. She had put this stuff behind her. *Face it, Jeannie, you are nothing but a promiscuous drunk!*

She quietly left the bed, found her clothes, and dressed in the dark. Without making a sound, she left and found her car outside the motel room. *Guess I must have followed him here,* she reasoned to herself. Checking her GPS, she drove back to the Holiday Inn with her aunt's statement about being her birth mother running through her head, not focusing on what had happened during the night.

Once in the hotel, she threw off her clothes and showered for what seemed like an hour to her, scrubbing every part of her body over and over. Wrapping herself in a towel, she assaulted her teeth with her toothbrush, ridding herself of any lingering taste, then plugged in the hotel room's coffee maker, knowing the brew would be strong. *Just what I need,* she thought.

The letters lying on the table called to her. After blowing her hair dry, she gathered them and the envelope, placed them in her purse, and went downstairs to the parking lot. She remembered the Waffle House location and drove to it. Finding an isolated table off to the side of the dining area, she waited for a cup of coffee and spread the documents on the table. There were no males in the restaurant and no sign of a new tail. She began to read.

> Jeannie, I led a wonderful and, at times, unladylike life when I was young. I felt I was a looker. At least that is what we called

ourselves back in my childhood if you felt better looking than other girls. I was a loose teenager, rebelling, I guess, using sex to become even more popular. My sister, your step-mom, was my exact opposite, and thank God for that. She was always good in school. Academically I held my own, but everything seemed to come naturally for her. We weren't rivals, but at the same time, it would be stretching it to say we were the best of friends.

I was eight years older than my sister. We didn't share the same friends. By the way, our family grew up in Myrtle Beach, which is where you are probably reading these letters. There is so much to tell you due to all these years apart, but knowing you have become an FBI agent, of which I am so proud, you probably want me to just get to the facts, right?

Jeannie caught herself smiling and continued to read.

During the Korean War, my sister and I fell in love with the same man. His name was Paul. Paul Radcliff. He was a handsome chap, and well, wouldn't you know it, my sister fell for his charms also, but she was too young, and I gave Paul all the attention he wanted if you know what I mean. I'm going to leave out the juicy parts, but as it turned out, I got pregnant. Pregnant with you, Jeannie. Can you image the disgrace I was bestowing on your grandparents? Both devote Catholics, and here, their oldest was pregnant out of wedlock.

Paul, your father, never knew I was pregnant. He was in the Air Force and was killed overseas before I could tell him. I am not feeling sorry for myself, but I found myself pregnant with a man that would never return to my life. My sister found another man, the one she later married who raised you as his daughter. You see, I confided with my sister that I was pregnant. She learned that I was going to have a friend use a coat hanger and, well, you know.

Instead, my sister, God bless her, proposed that we conceal my pregnancy. She and her husband, a great man, moved to California before your grandparents could notice signs of my pregnancy. He had no family, so moving was not a problem. He loved my sister so much that he agreed to take you in as their own once you were delivered.

Your birth came quicker than we expected, with me delivering you in my sister and husband's house in California. After a few weeks, I flew back to Myrtle Beach. I had to swear to my sister that I would never reveal what we had agreed to. We had to make my parents believe that my sister and husband had a beautiful baby girl. Shortly thereafter, both our parents, your grandparents, died. They, too, never got to see you.

Later, I married a very wealthy man. I told him about you, and he sincerely wanted to bring you back to South Carolina and be raised here. I refused and told him about my promise with my sister. Eventually, he dropped the subject. Shortly after your birth, I learned that I could not have any more children. So instead, he and I set out to establish a company that would be second to none.

I sent monthly stipends to my sister for your care, upbringing, and education. She would send me pictures, newspaper articles, and everything she could so that I might see you blossom into the woman you now are.

Please don't hate me, daughter. Yes, I regret what I did. I should have admitted my mistake and raised you here in Myrtle Beach with or without the possible scandal of my out-of-wedlock pregnancy. For that, I can never forgive myself. The rest of these letters express all the thoughts I had about you through these forty-something years. You might look at them as ramblings from an old woman, but I hope not. Throughout the days, months, and years, when I found my thoughts turning toward you,

I tried to record what I was thinking so that you knew you were always in my heart and soul.

Now, as you read this, I have left this world to join your father and my husband. I have left you the burden of a lifetime accumulation of wealth, for which I do not apologize. I know my sister raised you well and that you will do the right thing with what you have now inherited.

Besides the mansion that my husband and I built, you will have a considerable amount of cash and investments, including real estate. They are all listed somewhere in these documents. If you need any help whatsoever, contact Mr. Goldstein. I have worked with him for a long time, and I trust him implicitly.

If my cat is still alive, I hope you will maintain her care. She is getting up there in age, but if she is still with us, she outlived me, ha ha. I assume Isabel is taking care of her until you arrive. Please love her as much as I did. By the way, her name is Jeannie. Following the death of my husband, she was my closest companion. My final request is that when she passes, you sprinkle her ashes on my grave. My burial location has been included with these letters.

My sister and her husband loved you as if they had created you. I know I made the right decision in having them raise you. I loved you my whole life, Jeannie. My only sadness is not

being able to hold you and tell you in person.
Love, Mom.

Jeannie left the restaurant, emotionally drained. She made it back to her hotel room, where she immediately fell asleep from exhaustion.

Chapter Thirty

JEANNIE WOKE UP to a damp pillow smudged with makeup and mascara, still wearing the clothes she had on the day before. The letters were spread out on the desk and the spare bed. She was trying to figure out what her next move should be when her cellphone rang, startling her. It was Lomax.

"Hello, boss. How are you?" she answered.

"That's what I'm supposed to ask." Anyone tailing you?

"No."

"Well, for once since this whole mess started, I can give you some good news. It seems the Austrian government has reconsidered your extradition request. In fact, they're arranging for you to receive an award for your work in their country. Internal Affairs has exonerated you, and you'll receive official word later."

"What caused the turnaround, and what about the federal warrant for my arrest?"

"More good news. The deputy district attorney who got the warrant on you is now in federal custody. You were right. That left-wing piece of shit was bought and paid for by the Organization. We were able to get a wiretap on his cell and office phones and recorded tons of incriminating statements. He rolled over during interrogation and told us about the two cars that tailed you."

"The official word given for Austria's about-face is that their own investigation came to the same conclusion as our shooting board and that an apparent error resulted in your being erroneously accused of misconduct."

"That's the official word. What's the unofficial word?" Jeannie asked.

"Someone dropped a bomb on the president and members of the Austrian government bent on getting you back on their soil. Still don't know the motivation for it, but apparently, the president and some of her cabinet members liked to visit Mr. Epstein's island in the past for a little fun in the sun. To avoid the scandal this would cause if it were ever released, there was a quick about-turn." Lomax laughed. "So, how soon do you think you can get back in the saddle?"

"Would it be possible to have at least seven more days?"

"No. Take another two weeks, and I'll see you the following Monday. Let Flores have a little more glory in your absence. Do me a favor, however. Since the Organization was involved, continue to look over your shoulder, OK?"

The GPS seemed to become more confused the closer Jeannie got to the ocean. She crossed over from King's Highway to Ocean Blvd., but sometimes the guidance control instructed her to make a left turn that was blocked off by a concrete center divide. She passed numerous oceanfront condos, each seeming to be competing with the one next door to see which could be taller. In between the monoliths, she caught brief glimpses of the ocean. Tourists paraded the sidewalks, and mothers and fathers walked hand-in-hand with their children mixing with those who looked like the same dirtbags Jeannie saw in San Francisco, displaying butt cleavage with their pants hanging low on their hips.

Finally, she found the house, or did the house find her? Goldstein's statement that her aunt's house, actually her mother's house, was huge turned out to be an understatement; it covered three acres of oceanfront property. The primary residence was a beautiful three-story building with immaculate landscaping. The wrought iron gate was open when she arrived, and there was a Ford Prius that had seen better days parked at the end of the circular driveway near the entrance. Jeannie grabbed her purse and fished out the key to the front door. After climbing the brick stairs and approaching the oversized double front doors, they opened, and she was greeted by a woman whom Jeannie judged to be of Cuban descent on the basis of her accent.

"Hello. You must be Jeannie. I'm Isabel." She offered a warm, soft hand. "It is so nice to meet Sylvia's daughter after all these years. I would spend hours with her, and she would share your accomplishments. She always worried that you would be injured. She was very proud of you. Please come in and see your mother's home." Isabel was in her mid- to late-forties and overweight. Her once black hair now showed signs of gray. It appeared she had led a hard life. She was wearing a basic green Hawaiian moo-moo with palm tree designs.

Jeannie was still having problems with the "mother" reference, but her attention was diverted to a massive staircase rising from the marble floor. It dominated the grand entrance hall of etched mirrors. The staircase reminded Jeannie of the stairs in the movie *Titanic*, branching off at the top in opposite directions.

She heard the roar of the ocean and got her first real glimpse of the sea after following Isabel around the staircase. "Oh, this is Jeannie," she said, pointing to a large black cat stretched out like a rug in front of an enormous glass façade opening to the beach. "You know your mother named her after you, don't you?"

"My God. This is gorgeous," were the only words Jeannie could think of saying.

"Yes. Please follow me to your mother's favorite part of the house." Isabel opened French doors leading into a classic turn-of-the-century conservatory. Numerous Cymbidium orchids were located on watering tables, along with an outstanding collection of bonsai trees. Several waterfalls could be heard in the distance, drawing Jeannie's attention to a large koi pond with show-quality fish. Not surprisingly, the landscape around the pond was a Japanese garden.

Jeannie suddenly remembered she had to call Delores, her neighbor, to make sure her koi back home were OK. She then connected the fact that both she and her mom had a love of koi and Japanese gardens. She could not help but smile at the comforting idea.

"Your mother would sit here for hours on end, lost in thought. I would sometimes find her sleeping in that chair." Isabel began sniffling, pointing to a leather recliner. "I'm sorry. This is where I found her, you know, when she passed. That's the blanket she was using." Jeannie put her arms around Isabel, and they cried together.

"I just made a pot of coffee. Would you like some? We can drink out here."

"I'd like that." While waiting for Isabel to return, Jeannie found a decorative jar containing koi food and began feeding the fish who seemed to be starving. Jeannie felt a sense of calmness overcoming her. Was it the koi pond or the sight and sound of the ocean? Or was it the relief of knowing she was no longer a fugitive?

"Did you see the oceanfront condo buildings your mother owns on Ocean Boulevard?" Isabel asked as she poured coffee for her and Jeannie.

"Condo buildings? I didn't know she owned any, but I have only glanced at some of the investment documents she left me."

"Oh, yes. She has three. At one time, they were the biggest and finest on the Strand. After her first stroke, she began losing interest in them, calling them a bad investment. You know, she and her husband not only built one of them, but they lived there for several years on the beach while this place was being built. Your mother loved the ocean. She said the ocean provided a sense of nostalgia and a feeling of belonging and home."

Isabel gave Jeannie a quick tour of the house. It had eight bedrooms, five bathrooms, a library, game room, hot tub and sauna, and an outdoor swimming pool. *So long, Holiday Inn!*

Jeannie informed Isabel that she would be moving from her hotel to her mom's home but did not know her plans beyond the following week. She learned where and when to feed Jeannie the cat and asked Isabel to come for lunch the next day so Jeannie could learn more about the house and her mom.

Driving back to the hotel, Jeannie placed a call to agent Tim McGraw of the South Carolina Federal

Bureau of Investigation. He was not available, so she left her cellphone number. She quickly looked at the investment documents and wrote down the addresses of the three condo units on Ocean Blvd. Having packed her luggage and checked out of the hotel, she was picking up a chicken sandwich, fries, and drink at Bojangles and getting ready to search for the three buildings when her phone rang.

"Jeannie. How are you?" asked agent McGraw.

"Fine, Tim, and you?" She had met him when they both attended a briefing in Quantico. There, she learned of his specialty in real estate fraud.

"Can't complain. No one will listen. What can I do you out of?"

"What can you tell me about those oceanfront condo units on Ocean Boulevard?" she asked.

"Tell me you're planning on renting a unit, not buying one."

"Well, a friend of mine was thinking of buying one and asked my opinion. I told her I didn't know anything about condo purchases or timeshares but that I'd contact a friend who's an expert in real estate and would find out?"

"Expert, huh? Tell that to Washington, and maybe I'll get a raise! Fat chance of that. OK, in a nutshell, to rent, depending on where on Ocean Boulevard you want to stay, just check around until you find one you like. They're pretty much laid out the same. Those with a full ocean view are going to cost you more, depending on how many rooms it has. The farther away from the arcades, the fewer fun things there are to do, but also fewer assholes on the street. You won't see them when they're urinating or defecating in the alleys."

"Now, to buy one, stay away. They're money pits. Many are in bad physical shape, and when repairs have to be made, the homeowners association passes it down the line. I could go on and on, but as an investment, you'll lose.

"Damn! That means the owners are either forced to take it in the shorts or sell, I guess?"

"Yeah, but most mortgage companies are well aware of those buildings having major problems, so unless a seller finds a person with cash who doesn't do their due diligence, you're stuck."

Chapter Thirty-one

ARNOLD PACED BACK and forth in his basement, wearing out the rug. Between visions of those he had tortured in this very room and the terror of police closing in on him, the urge to kill grew. He even entertained thoughts of killing his wife and children and then disappearing into the Idaho wilderness. Thinking he had good survival skills, he could, on occasion, venture into civilization, select some prey, and hunt.

Some cops looked at him differently in the bakery. Some, however, told him how he should sue the bitch for defamation. He laughed off their suggestions. The next kill would take all his energy and concentration. His wife would be taking their kids to visit relatives in seven days. He would try a dry run just to see if the cops had a tail on him. The following day would be the time to see if he was being watched.

***

Jeannie had lunch delivered to her mom's house before Isabel arrived. Nothing fancy, just sandwiches cut into triangles, a small Caesar salad for two, and two slices of cheesecake. She found her way around the spacious kitchen and prepared a pot of coffee. By then, she had already gotten got lost in the house three times. *Come on, girl. You're supposed to be a highly trained FBI agent.* She thought Ismail would be saying something like that to her if he knew what was happening. Little Jeannie the cat ignored her and was eating the cat food in her dish; Jeannie took that as a good sign.

Isabel arrived at 11:45. Instead of entering unannounced, she knocked on the door, which Jeannie thought was nice. The transition of the property had already taken place in Isabel's mind. Before lunch, Jeannie told her about getting lost in the mansion, and Isabel asked if she would like to be given a more proper tour and learn the ins and outs of the place. Jeannie could not resist. In the process, Isabel told stories of the house's construction, the many parties her mom and her husband had held in the ballroom, and how little Jeannie still believes she owns the house. In fact, she followed them from room to room during the tour.

They returned to the conservatory and ate around the koi pond. At the conclusion of lunch, Jeannie excused herself and returned with several large envelopes. "Isabel, first, thank you so much for taking care of my mom these last few years. I'm sure it put a burden on you and your family." Isabel waved her hand, brushing off the compliment. "I hope you'll not become offended by what I'm about to offer you. This is all new to me. I mean, this house, this new-found wealth—I still haven't gotten a handle on it.

"I need to return to San Francisco and will return several more times after I figure out what I'm going to do. With that in mind, I won't be driving on those occasions. This old girl needs to just strap herself into a plane and let someone else do the driving, so to speak." Isabel laughed.

She handed Isabel an envelope. "I want you and your husband to buy a new car."

"I don't understand. My old car gets us around," she said with a beleaguered and shocked expression.

"Understood. But I hope you'll continue to take care of this home and little Jeannie in my absence, and that will require you to come and go, putting wear and tear on your Prius. Plus, if you don't mind, I'd like you to pick me up when I fly here instead of relying on Uber or a cab. I'll let you know way in advance so you can schedule me in. I hope that'll be OK?"

"Jeannie, I can do that in my old car. You don't have to give me money for a new one."

"My mind is made up. Take the money and get a great car for you and the family. Everyone can use a second car. Next, I contacted a friend who's an FBI agent specializing in real estate fraud and asked him about the large condo complexes my mom owned. She was right about them being a bad investment. The older they get, the more of a financial drain they become. I contacted Mr. Goldstein, my mom's estate attorney. Do you know him? Oh wait, you already told me you did."

"Yes. He's a very kind man. Your mother trusted him completely."

"Although his expertise is not in real estate, he has contacts with other attorneys well versed in real estate transactions. I've signed off on one of those complexes and transferred ownership to you and your family. You can keep it if you wish, although you might consider selling it and investing the money for your children's education and for a rainy day. Here is Mr. Goldstein's business card. He'll contact you in a few days and go over everything with you and your husband and set you up with a realtor and attorney should you wish to sell. I've already retained Mr. Goldstein and arranged for his service and the services of others, so you and your husband won't have any expenses."

Jeannie then lied. "It was my mom's last request that you and your family be taken care of, so you can't refuse."

Isabel began crying uncontrollably. "Your mother will always be in my heart, Jeannie."

"Yes, well, here's the deed for the condo building." She handed Isabel the second envelope. "By the way, I passed by it yesterday on my way to pick up my stuff from the hotel. It's a big one. Good luck with your decision."

"Now, this envelope contains my personal check. Use these funds for any expenses you incur on the upkeep of the house. The sum also includes fees for service. Here's my business card. Feel free to call me anytime, day or night, for anything. My mother and I cannot repay you enough."

***

Jeannie had taken the southern route to South Carolina and decided the northern route might to fun on her return trip to California, hopefully without a tail. After a final call to Goldstein's office, she made quick stops to see the other two condo buildings on Ocean Blvd. *Let's see what this looks like on the inside,* she thought to herself as she approached the building.

Upon entering, she smelled chlorine and assumed there must be an indoor pool close by. The reception area was clean, but it showed wear. No one was at the desk. Tourist season had passed. There was a restaurant, a Starbucks, and a souvenir shop on the main floor, but they were all closed. She imaged how crowded it must be when summer arrives.

She located the elevator banks and called the car. When it arrived at the lobby level, she entered and pressed the button for the top floor. Upon exiting, she was overcome by the smell of what she would describe as "oldness." The carpet on the floor of a somewhat narrow hallway was clean, but the wear of heavy foot traffic was obvious. A maid cleaning a room had propped the door open with her cart, giving Jeannie a chance to look inside. It appeared to be a small apartment with a sleeper couch, small kitchen table, two-burner stove, small refrigerator, and a flat-screen TV mounted on the wall. A large sliding glass door provided an ocean view. She returned to the lobby and walked to the other complex next door.

A black female in cornrows was sitting at the front desk listening to her cellphone and did not look up when Jeannie approached the elevators. Three elderly women were seated in an alcove off the lobby on high-back chairs. One was knitting, and the other two were reading. The entire wall to their side was made of glass, providing a stunning view of the ocean.

Jeannie entered the elevator and again chose the top floor as her destination. Around the ninth floor, the elevator quickly jolted and came to a stop. She held onto the small bar around the inside of the car, waiting for the elevator to jolt again and resume its ascent. It did not. She pressed the alarm, and a siren went off. *Oh, that's just great!*

She picked up the elevator phone and placed a call. A female answered. Jeannie assumed it was the girl at the desk. "Hello, are you aware that the elevator has stopped on the 9th floor?" she asked.

"Again?" the receptionist asked. "Don't panic. It happens all the time. The fire department will be here before you know it."

Jeannie grabbed her cellphone and placed a call. "Jeannie, you are up bright and early today. Heading home, are you?" Goldstein asked.

"Yes, not yet packed but ready to see the top half of the United States. Currently, I'm trapped in an elevator in one of my mom's high risers. Yes, the receptionist told me the fire department should be here soon. Two things: I gave the deed to Isabel for one of the high risers. Looks like my stopping to look at the other two was a bad idea. Please expedite the sale of them both."

***

Delaney was amazed at how easy it was to make his decision. He realized in his conversation with Mr. Brown that he was most happy as a loner with an occasional love affair. That would not be fair to Jeannie. His only regret was not being able to tell her that he would be disappearing permanently. At least his anonymous phone call to the Austrian government resolved the ridiculous matter of extradition, and now Jeannie could get back to her life. He wondered how the Special Service Branch would erase him.

***

George Arnold waved goodbye to his family as they drove off, hardly able to control his excitement. As usual, he opened the bakery and worked until dusk. Before locking up for the day, he removed a floor tile near the oven and pulled out a handgun. Just another boring day, he hoped the cops would think if they were watching. Securing the door, he headed for home, unaware Jeannie was watching his every move.

So far, so good, he thought. At daybreak, he got up, had breakfast, and tossed a duffel bag of beef jerky, a thermos of coffee, crackers, and a few power bars into the car. After backing out of the driveway, he drove around his immediate neighborhood to see if he could spot a tail. Seeing none, he set out for the airport, prepped his plane, and took off. Once in the air, he circled the airfield several times with an eye out for surveillance cars being concealed. Again, he failed to see anything to suggest he was being watched. Taking the thermos from the duffle bag, he poured himself a cup of coffee. The coast was clear. Tomorrow, he would be able to hunt. His surveillance flight over, he smiled all the way home in anticipation of his next kill.

Once back in the house, he removed two pieces of wall paneling halfway up the staircase and pulled out a rifle he had wrapped in a blanket. He grabbed the chains, replaced the rifle, and headed to the basement.

That was all he remembered when he woke up. A blindfold over his eyes prevented him from seeing anything. His hands and wrists were wrapped in a cloth material with nylon cuffs, securing him to a chair. His feet were secured in a similar fashion. He tried to free himself, and that is when she spoke.

"Arnold, don't make me hit you again. You'll not be able to break the cuffs. So, this is where you bring all your victims. You're a sick puppy, aren't you? But a clever one. How many poor women did you kill during your pathetic lifetime, huh? Twenty, thirty, more? And your wife—she doesn't know what a sick bastard you are, does she?

"It's a myth that most serial killers want to be caught. Most, like you, don't, and few ever express remorse. They have what I call a black heart. In rare instances, they do express remorse, but mostly hoping it'll get them a lesser sentence. What about you, Arnold? Now that you're caught, will you show remorse? Will you show remorse for the lives you ended?

"The police, in my opinion, have an excellent case against you, but sometimes the law prevents them from doing what's right. You know, not enough evidence for a search warrant, or a bleeding-heart liberal district attorney, or a judge who has a soft spot for animals like you.

"I once had a professor who told us to envision justice as a pendulum; when it swings too far to the right, we have totalitarianism, you know, like Hitler, Mussolini, Saddam Hussain, but if the pendulum swings too far to the left, we'll get what's happening in some cities today, lawlessness, anarchy, and lack of accountability.

"Parasites like you blend into their surroundings, using it to spot their prey. Then, as a sociopath, they create an elaborate plan to satisfy their depraved desires. And who did you pick for your victims, Arnold? Society's castaways. Prostitutes, strippers, runaways. Women who, after you selected them, were tortured and then transported in your plane to a wilderness area where you, the great hunter, tracked them down and shot them with your high-powered rifle.

"You hoped they'd never be found. In the event they were, who'd care, right? Society would be better off without them." Arnold struggled with his bindings, sweating profusely, snot running from his nose.

"Everything went great for years, didn't it? First Alaska, then Iowa, and now here in Idaho, or did it begin earlier in your life? Were you a bedwetter, Arnold? Did you like to torture animals, maybe cut them up?

"Yes, you were clever, but one escaped, didn't she? I understand that you kept your cool. The cops couldn't find any evidence here. Who's going to believe a prostitute over you, a successful business owner? By the way, where do you keep your kill kit, Arnold?" Arnold continued to squirm, but the cuffs were on tight. Without the cloth acting as a barrier, he was sure his wrists would be bleeding.

"You might be asking yourself who I am? That doesn't matter. What matters is whether you are going to be remorseful. You probably hoped that if you got caught, some technicality would get you off. I'm here to make sure that doesn't happen."

"Who are you? How'd you get into my house? Get out before I call the cops."

"Oh, that's pretty rich, George. You, who killed—how many young women? Now you want the police to come and save your sorry ass. Okay, let's get the party started. You'll tell me where your rifle and other instruments of your trade are located. Next, we'll try to reconstruct all your kills and where you left their bodies."

"Fuck you, bitch. Take these cuffs off me, and I'll show you my rifle, you cunt."

"Georgie, Georgie, is that any way to talk to a lady? Which rifle are you talking about? You mean this pathetic little dick you have hanging between your legs?"

Arnold tried as hard as he could but could not overcome his bindings. He heard the woman pick something up from a table and open and close it. He knew from the sound it was a pair of scissors. "Let's see what you have down there. Many serial killers have small penises and can't get them up if they try. Is that your problem?"

She cut his pants off and then his underwear. "Oh, my God!" she said, laughing. "You poor guy, or should

I say, your poor wife." She then cut off his shirt and t-shirt, leaving him naked.

"From what I've read in police reports, you somehow pick your victims up randomly. I disagree. I think you have a particular type that turns you on, you pervert. All your victims are short to average. Not an obese one in the bunch. You like long hair, huh? Then, after you have fun with them at your house, you get them in your plane and fly them out to the wildness where the real fun starts, isn't that right?" She slapped him on the back of his head.

Arnold felt the tip of the scissors touch the center of his chest. "It would be easy to just slit your throat and let you bleed out, but that's too easy. Where's the fun in that, right? Plus, we have much to discuss. How about we start here?" One side of the scissors touched his right testicle. He tried to jump and urinated on himself. "Uh oh, someone peed on himself.

"Now, here's how my game is played. I'll ask you a question, you'll answer, and we'll move on to the next. If you decide to be an asshole and spoil my game, then you'll either get a nice deep cut somewhere, or you'll lose something." She touched his testicle again with the scissors.

Chapter Thirty-two

"Are you on your way back?" Ismail asked as Jeannie was approaching a rest area along the Oregon coast.

"Hang on; I need to turn down my radio. Ah, you missed me. Yes, I'm in Oregon now. I hope to get home by late this evening. Lomax told me to come in on Monday, so I can have a few days to recuperate."

"Don't get all mushy on me. I just needed to know so I can clean my stuff out of your office. Of course, the hot tub and flatscreen will have to stay. So, how was the vacation? I hear the Austrians got off your ass, and you're no longer a wanted felon."

"Yeah, but I still don't understand why they targeted me. Lomax said I might never find out. The vacation was nice. I got to see a lot of the country I'd always wanted to see."

"That's good. Well, it's time for you to earn your keep. I'll have a coffee waiting for you on Monday." Not waiting for a response, he hung up. Still smiling, her cell rang again.

"Jeannie, it's Sgt. Elders. You'll never guess what happened. Do you have a few minutes?

"Sure, I'm just pulling into a rest stop in Oregon. Can you hear me? Let me park."

Elders could get so excited that sometimes he had to pause and come up for air. "OK, what's up?"

"George Arnold killed himself," he blurted.

"What? When?"

"His wife came home from visiting her family and found him in the basement. He'd shot himself in the head; did it with a wooden-handled .357 magnum. He left a suicide note saying he couldn't live like this anymore and admitted to killing over thirty-nine women. He kept a journal of all his kills. The sick fuck even left a crude map showing where he discarded them, but I don't know if we'll find any remains after this long period. He also wrote about where to find the rifle. Two pieces of removable paneling by the stairs concealed the rifle and chains he used to bind his victims. We found those and jewelry that were apparently his trophies. Can you believe it?" Jeannie just smiled and shook her head.

Jeannie pushed her garage door opener and parked her sports car, but not fast enough to avoid Delores, her loving, snoopy neighbor. "Hi, Jeannie, you're back!

How was the trip? Your fish are fine. I checked them twice a day. Oh, and we made sure your garbage can was put out the first week you were gone." Delores also never came up for air. Jeannie immediately thought of a noted similarity between her and Isabel. *Yep, I bet Delores would take care of me as well as Isabel took care of my mom.*

Once Jeannie had unpacked the car, she showered, changed into her sweats, and decided to call Delaney. In the past, her calls went to voice messaging. She had heard on the news that the Black Cell had been successfully eliminated. *So, why hasn't he called?* She wondered. All she heard was, "We're sorry. The number you are trying to reach is no longer in service. Please check your number and try again." *What the hell?*

Coming this fall:

The Phantom Train

A Jeannie Loomis Novel

A mother and teenage daughter's bodies are found on the Presidio grounds in San Francisco, both brutally tortured and killed. Jeannie and her team take over the investigation of a double homicide, like those they have worked numerous times in the past. Little did they know that these murders would involve them in one of history's greatest mysteries: the location of Hitler's Secret Gold Train.

www.ingramcontent.com/pod-product-compliance
Lightning Source LLC
Chambersburg PA
CBHW060550310726
48982CB00008B/1072/J

* 9 7 8 1 7 3 7 8 7 3 6 2 4 *